THE
PICKLE SONG

THE PICKLE SONG

Barthe DeClements

VIKING

I wish to express my thanks to
Denise Ohlson
and her students at Machias Elementary
for sharing their school experiences with me.

CONTENTS

Shifty Eyes

Casey flipped a thumb at Bitsey. "What's that thing supposed to be?"

"A Pomeranian," I told him. "My grandma thinks it's a dog."

Bitsey was sniffing around in the tall grass by the creek and Casey gave her a nudge with his boot. "What are you doing with it?"

"I'm supposed to be taking her out for air."

"Air? Is that what you call it?"

Bitsey pulled on the leash, nosing closer and closer to the creek. I yanked her back. "We're not going in the water, stupid. My shoes are already wet from standing in the grass waiting for you."

"I could take care of your problem easy," Casey said with a grin.

"Ya, how?"

He tilted his head toward the road. "Just hold her by the tail and swing her around a telephone pole a couple times."

"No, I don't want to hear my grandma scream."

"Can't help you then, Paula." Casey turned and walked up to the road and headed toward his house.

His house is a small shacky place. His stepbrothers hang out in the yard with their sleeves rolled up, showing off their tattoos. The oldest one has a motorcycle. They take turns piling on it and screeching down the road.

One night, when they roared up and down our street at eleven-thirty, my mom called the cops. Casey asked me at school the next day if I knew who'd turned them in. I shrugged and pretended I'd been sound asleep the whole night. I'm not dumb enough to get his brothers mad at my mom.

After Casey left for his house, I followed Bitsey while she poked along the creek's edge. About half a block downstream, I spied a girl leaning over the water. There are plenty of boys in my neighborhood, but there aren't any girls. Except maybe the new girl in my sixth grade, Sukey Parsons.

She'd only been in the class two days and her desk was across the room, so I'd barely talked to her. Not in school anyway.

Thursday afternoon, I'd seen her get off the bus two blocks before my house and go into the woods. Friday afternoon, as we lined up to get on the bus, I asked, "Did you just move in near the Machias Road? That's where I live."

"I'm not sure." Her brown eyes darted to the left and then right. "I'm not sure of my address yet." She hurried up the bus steps and sat in a seat next to a third grader. I sat in back and tried to figure out why she was shifty-eyed.

Bitsey pulled on her leash. There was a bush a few feet away that she wanted to smell. I let her because it gave me a better view of the girl who had her head in the creek. I was wondering if the girl could be Sukey when she stood up and wrapped a towel around her hair. That's who it was all right.

"Hi!" I called out.

Sukey's hands froze on the towel. I didn't know if she was going to run or say hello back. She did both. "Oh. Hi," she said and scurried up the bank to the road.

When I arrived home with Bitsey, Grandma and Mom were sitting on the couch having cake and coffee. Grandma likes to eat and it shows. You can't tell where her chest ends and her stomach starts.

The first thing she asked me was, "Did Bitsey do her job?"

"Who knows," I said. "She's so tiny I can't tell if she's squatting or standing."

Grandma frowned. "Well, you can see her legs, can't you?"

"Not if she's in the grass by the creek, I can't. And that's where she insisted on going."

"Oh, Itsey Bitsey, you obstinate baby." Grandma picked up her dog to hug her.

"Her tummy's all wet," she told me.

"That's nothing. Look at my tennis shoes."

This time Mom frowned. "I don't want you getting another cold. Take them off and put them in the dryer."

I went in the kitchen to drop my shoes in the dryer and then went to my bedroom to hang up my jacket. I came back to the living room in my slippers. "Can I have some cake now?"

"Get yourself a glass of milk and a plate and I'll cut you a piece," Mom said.

The cake was good. Carrot with a cream cheese frosting. I asked Grandma if she made it. She just nodded. She was busy petting Bitsey, who was squirming around in her lap.

I leaned forward in my chair. "Mom, I think there's a new girl in the neighborhood, but she acts weird."

"How weird?"

"Well, every time I try to talk to her, she cuts me off. I saw her get off the bus ahead of my stop and asked her if she lived around here. She said she didn't know her address. And then today I saw her down by the creek washing her hair. I said hi and she said hi and then she split."

"Maybe she's shy," Mom said. "It would be nice for you to have a girlfriend. Be friendly to her."

"I am being friendly," I insisted, "but—"

Grandma let out a squeal. "Bitsey! No! No!" she shoved Bitsey on the floor, grabbed a napkin, and frantically mopped at the puddle in her lap.

"This dress just came back from the cleaners!" she wailed. "Paula, I told you to take Bitsey out so she could go."

"I tried," I said, picking up my empty plate and glass and heading for the kitchen, fast. I kicked the door closed behind me so Grandma couldn't hear me laughing.

After Grandma left to drive back to Seattle, Mom opened the Saturday mail I'd brought in. "Oh, my heavens, the homeowner's insurance is due next month. I forgot all about it. How am I going to pay that?"

She looked up at me as if she expected an answer. Instead, I reached out to the coffee table to pick up the *TV Guide.*

She flipped through the other envelopes. "All bills and advertisements. Nothing from your father, of course."

"I think the mill is only going three days a week now." I kept my voice as neutral as possible. If Mom thought I was sticking up for Dad, it could start a big fight.

"The least he could do is send half of what he owes," she said sharply. "He's probably spending it at the tavern with that bevel sawyer. Or maybe she's cut off the rest of her fingers and he has to support her, too."

"I better do my homework." I put the *TV Guide* back on the table and headed for my bedroom. I planned to stay there until she cooled down about the bills. After she did, she'd probably call up Grandma and ask for a loan.

While the mill was going full-time, Dad had paid support money for me every month. Then the spotted owl got endangered and people got upset about Washington forests being clear-cut and logging sites were closed so there wasn't much wood coming into sawmills. Anyway, that's the way Dad explained it to me. He said he was looking for another job, but not to say anything to Mom until he had one.

I try to be friends with both my parents. That isn't too easy because Mom's bitter about the bevel sawyer.

The night she found out about her was the worst night of Mom's life, I think.

Dad hadn't come home for dinner, and by ten o'clock she was sure he was dead on Highway 9. That was two years ago. Mom didn't want to leave me home because I was only nine years old then. She put me in the backseat of our car with a blanket and took off for the town of Arlington.

There were no wrecks on Highway 9. When we got to the mill in Arlington, it was dark and empty. Mom drove to a tavern to ask the bartender if anybody had seen my dad.

I huddled under my blanket while she went inside. It seemed as if she was in there a long time. When she did come out, she was crying and screaming. Dad was running after her, trying to stop her by grabbing at her arm. She hit him in the face, called him a bunch of names, wrenched open the door of our car, and roared out of the tavern's parking lot. She drove like mad all the way home, crying the whole time. I was scared silly.

After she got in the house, she threw herself on the couch and sobbed and sobbed. I climbed up beside her and patted her curly hair, trying to make her feel better. She hugged me and told me to go to bed. I did, with my cheek wet from being squeezed against her wet cheek.

In the morning, while I ate my breakfast and got ready for school, Mom packed Dad's clothes. When I got home, his closet was empty. I looked. And none of his other things were around either.

Mom never told me what happened in the tavern. I guessed the bevel sawyer and Dad were in there together. Maybe dancing or kissing. Mom just said she and Dad were separated and Dad was going to live in Arlington by his work.

The first time I visited Dad for a weekend, I half expected to meet a woman in his little apartment. I looked around there, too, but there weren't any female clothes hanging in his closet. I asked him if he was going to get married again. He laughed and said, "Not a chance."

When I got home, Mom tried to find out how Dad was living. She asked me sneaky questions like "What did you and your dad do?" and "Did someone go to the movies with you?" After about a year she came right out and made cracks about the bevel sawyer.

I've only seen the bevel sawyer a few times. She came by Rotten Ralph's one Sunday morning when Dad and I were having breakfast there. He introduced her to me and I found out her name is Leslie. I asked her what bevel sawyers do.

"Saw the beveled edge on the hip and ridge," she said.

I must have looked puzzled because she ran her stumpy fingers through her short blond hair before she explained, "The sides of wood planks are usually square, right?"

"Right," I said.

"I put a diagonal edge on them. Then two of the pieces are nailed together to make the peak of a shake roof."

"But how do you put the edge on the wood?" I asked.

"By guiding the lumber through a buzz saw."

"Oh," I said. That's not something I ever plan to do.

While I was remembering the bevel sawyer's three fingers cut off at the second knuckles, I was stretched out on my bed. Mom's voice in the living room interrupted my thoughts. I guessed she was on the phone talking Grandma into a loan and it was safe for me to come out.

Before I could get off the bed, Mom opened my door. "How come you're not doing your homework?"

"I was wondering," I said. "Doesn't it seem strange that a girl would be washing her hair in the creek at the end of September?"

"Yes, it does." Mom looked thoughtful a moment. "Maybe her family's building a house and they're living in a small trailer on the lot. Two of my friends did that to save money. But I think if you don't have the septic tank in, it's illegal. Maybe that's why the girl doesn't want to give out her address."

"Maybe," I said.

Wild Animal

On the first day of sixth grade, Mom'd said she was tired of my whining about what she made for my lunch. From then on, I had to make it myself. I should have knocked off the whining in the fifth grade.

She used to put Oreos and Jell-O pudding in my lunch sack. You can get anything you want from the other kids if you have Oreos. This year Mom said if I wanted cookies, I could make them. I did, but they weren't very good and no one would trade.

The Monday after I'd seen Sukey at the creek, I

said to Mom, "I don't see why you can't buy me cookies. I never complained about those."

"You're not helpless," Mom said. "If you want dessert, get an apple off the tree in the backyard. That's what I've got."

"That's what you have because you're afraid of getting fat."

She folded down the top of her lunch sack, picked up her purse, and gave me a kiss on my forehead. "An apple a day keeps the doctor away."

I'd practiced twisting my lips in the mirror. But the sneer didn't bother her. She sailed out the door to her car.

I went in the backyard. It took me a while to find an apple without a scab or a bird bite in it. I almost missed my bus.

We eat our lunches in our classroom. When Mr. Loyal finishes his, he walks around the room and talks to the kids. This Monday, he stopped at Sukey's desk. "No milk or juice for you? Aren't you going to get thirsty?"

Sukey had been eating a cinnamon roll and she kept it up to her mouth while she shook her head. Mr. Loyal must have known she was embarrassed. Even though her head was down, I could see her cheeks turn pink.

He gave her a pat on the shoulder and walked on to John's and Spencer's desks. They were fiddling with their science project. Mr. Loyal pulled up a chair and helped them get the wires attached to their batteries and light bulb.

On Tuesday, I noticed that Sukey ate cinnamon rolls again. She and I were in the same tetherball game at recess. She's good at games and so am I. On the way back to the school building, we talked about what a poor loser Karen is. "She stamps away like that every time she doesn't win," I told Sukey.

I'd have liked to talk to her some more on the bus, but she sat down with somebody else again. "Sukey's sure hard to make friends with," I told Mom.

That night, the neighbor's dog made a big fuss. He never barks unless something is really going on. After he kept it up for half an hour, I was awake, Mom was awake, and so were the neighbors. Mom got up to get her flashlight before she saw Mr. Willmore out in the backyard with his.

While I was on the toilet, Mom came in the bathroom to wait her turn. "I don't know why a prowler would come around here," I said. "We haven't got anything to steal and neither do the Willmores."

"Maybe it was one of those pesky raccoons," Mom said.

Saturday, Mom announced that she and I were making applesauce to freeze for the winter. My first job was to pick the apples. As soon as I finished my breakfast, I got the basket and went out to the trees.

There was no use stalling around. If I did, I'd just have to listen to a long lecture about money and bills and the cost of food. And at the end, she'd be sure to throw in something about my dad and the support payments.

I finished the first tree in about ten minutes. I was thinking there weren't many apples left on it. There weren't many on the other tree either.

"Is that all you picked?" Mom said after I came in.

"That's all there is. The raccoons must have eaten them."

"They can't climb to the end of the branches!" She put on her sweater and went out in the backyard with me following her.

"See," I said.

Mom shook her head. "I can't believe the raccoons did that."

While I peeled the apples, I remembered Sukey's Friday lunch. I had looked across the room to see if she was eating cinnamon rolls again without anything to drink. She wasn't. She was eating apples.

That wasn't too weird. Lots of kids bring fruit in their lunch sacks. It was just that I didn't see her eating anything else.

The first three days of the next week, she ate more apples. I cleaned out my desk and took my time tossing the gum wrappers and crumpled papers into the wastebasket so I could sneak glance at Sukey's red apples. Sure enough, they had scabs and bird bites in them. And they were round at the bottom instead of bumpy like the store ones are.

I planned to talk to Mom about this on the way to the orthodontist Wednesday. We were two blocks from our house when she pointed out a tan car. "That car's been parked there for weeks," she said. "I've seen it every morning on my way to work."

"Mom, that car's right by the creek where I saw Sukey Parsons washing her hair. And Sukey's been eating apples that look like the ones in our yard."

"How do you know?" Mom asked.

"Because I thought it was funny she only had apples for lunch so I took a good look at them."

Mom turned up the road toward Frontier Village. Two of Casey's stepbrothers zoomed past us on their motorcycle.

"Those boys should be gotten off the street," Mom muttered. "The police never patrol these back roads."

I said, "Mom, if Sukey only has our apples to eat, maybe her family is homeless."

"No, I don't think a homeless family would come way out to Lake Stevens. I think they stay around Seattle or maybe Everett."

Everett's where our orthodontist is. I couldn't get Mom interested in talking about Sukey the rest of the way there or back. Mom doesn't have much imagination. Dad does. It makes him fun to be around.

I stay with Dad every other weekend. I had my bag packed early Saturday morning and was waiting in the living room for the sound of his truck. That's when Mom came in from the kitchen and dumped the load about Grandma on me.

"Paula, your grandma's coming to stay with us," she said.

"For how long?"

Mom was still in her bathrobe and she concentrated on retying her belt. "She's moving in."

"*What!*" I almost fell off the couch.

"It'll be good for all of us. We'll get help with the bills and she'll have some company."

"She's got company," I said. "She lives with two other teachers."

"Well, I'm not sure she's happy with them."

I bet they weren't happy with her either. "We only have two bedrooms. She isn't sleeping with me."

"No," Mom said. "We're giving her your room and you're moving in mine."

"No way! You snore."

"I do not snore. And I'm not trusting your smart mouth with your grandma. You can move your things in my room when you get home Sunday."

"You're just telling me this now to spoil my weekend with Dad."

"I'm telling you so you'll get used to the idea and not throw a fit when your grandma arrives. And whose fault is it, anyway, that I can't pay for this house all by myself?" Mom turned and went back in the kitchen. She always sees to it that she isn't in the living room when Dad knocks on the door.

I sat on the couch, steaming. She wasn't going to blackmail me into making a big scene with Dad. It wasn't his fault that the shake mill was running part-time.

I had myself almost calm by the time Dad arrived. I planned to start our ride to Arlington by talking about Sukey instead of Grandma and money. It turned out that Dad agreed with me that Sukey's family could be homeless.

"If you're living out of your car, parking on a back road by woods and a creek is a pretty good idea. Especially if fruit trees are nearby." Dad turned off Highway 92 and onto 9. "What does this Sukey look like?"

"She wears jeans and T-shirts like the other kids do." The T-shirt I was wearing that day had printing on the back: Women Can Run the World. Mom gave it to me, of course.

"Sukey's hair is long like mine, only straighter and darker," I went on. "She has brown eyes, too, but hers slant up at the ends. She's kinda pale and thin. She reminds me of a wild animal, maybe a fox, because she stops to stare through those slanted eyes and then disappears into the woods."

"Interesting person to get to know," Dad said.

"But that isn't easy." I explained to him how Sukey always chose a seat on the bus with someone else.

"Her parents might have told her not to let anyone find out where she stays. They have to have an address in the district where their kids go to school."

"Her mom probably made up one for the principal," I guessed.

Dad nodded. "Keep your eyes open. She'll be walking to the store or the post office one of these days and you can join her. Take it slow. Don't rush it and you'll make friends with her."

He smiled down at me and, for the first time that day, I noticed it was sunny out. We had lunch at Rotten Ralph's. Cheeseburgers.

That night we went to a movie. When we got back to his apartment, he helped me pull out the living room couch to make my bed. I almost asked him if I could live with him all the time, but he only has one tiny closet in his dinky bedroom. There really isn't any place for my stuff.

Our old house has a huge basement. Before I fell asleep, I thought about making a room for myself down there. If Dad boarded up a third of it and I painted the cement floor, it might look okay. At least I wouldn't be sleeping with Mom.

Sunday morning, we ate at Rotten Ralph's again. While I smeared jelly on my toast, I said, "Mom snores."

Dad burst into a laugh and spilled coffee out of the cup he was holding.

"She claims she doesn't," I told him. "And I have to sleep in her room because Grandma's coming to live with us."

Dad quickly picked up his paper napkin and wiped off the table. I knew he was trying to be careful about what he said next. "Your grandma has a dog."

"Come on, Dad. Get real. That thing isn't a dog!"

He shot me a sneaky grin.

"Dad, she'll drive me nuts."

"I know, honey. She drives everybody nuts. I don't think she's ever taught in one high school more than two years. Those principals take turns dumping her on each other."

I knew Grandma was always changing schools, but I didn't know it was because the principals got rid of her. That part was news to me.

Dad put out his big hand and laid it over mine. "Listen, Paula, I'm sorry I can't do anything for you now. I'm trying, but nothing's come through for me yet."

He was so sad and serious, I hurried to assure him. "That's all right. That's all right. I don't need anything big. I just thought maybe you could find some extra wood for me."

"Wood?"

"Maybe some scrap lumber. Do you think you could find some and build a wall in the basement? So I could have a room down there?"

"You want me to build a partition for you? Is this okay with your mother?"

I threw out my arms, almost knocking over my orange juice. "Oh, do we always have to do what Mom wants? Can't you just build me a room?"

"Sure I can," he said. "We'll build it next weekend."

"Aw right!"

On the way home, I was still feeling happy. I didn't even cringe when Grandma arrived and gave me a puckery kiss. And all night while Mom snored, I kept saying to myself, "I only have to listen to this for a week."

The Cold Hard Face

I usually blurt out news as soon as I get it. I kept my mouth shut about the basement, though. Monday morning I just yawned a lot, rubbed my eyes, and could hardly finish my breakfast. "For heaven's sake, sit up straight," Grandma snapped. "You look like an old lady."

"I can't. I'm tired," I moaned.

Grandma turned to Mom. "You weren't allowed to stay up past nine until you were thirteen years old. Why don't you give Paula an earlier bedtime?"

"We get up at six-thirty," I said, remembering to keep a whine in my voice. "I can't stay in bed for nine and a half hours."

"Well, you obviously aren't getting enough sleep," Grandma said.

"That's because Mom's snoring keeps waking me up."

Mom had known what was coming and she already had an exasperated look on her face. "I *do not* snore."

"Yes, you do," Grandma corrected her. "You've snored since you were a baby. I think there's something wrong with your nose."

"Why didn't you have it fixed then?" Mom got up from the table and marched into her room for her coat. When she came back, she ordered me to clean the kitchen before I went to school. She barely touched my cheek with her goodbye kiss. But I figured if my war plans got me a basement room, it would be worth her being a little bit mad.

I made her even madder the next morning. She'd strung a clothesline across the side of her room for the things we wore during the week. Our best clothes and grubbies took up the space in her closet.

When I pulled my pink blouse down from the line, I gave the hanger an extra hard yank. Mom was putting on her pantyhose and she looked up as the line broke from the hook on the wall and all the clothes slid to the floor. "Paula Tomlin! You did that on purpose."

I dropped my blouse on the bed and hurried to get the stool from in front of her dresser. I placed the stool under the wall hook, picked up the rope, and climbed on the stool.

"Get down," she demanded. "I'll do that."

I handed her the rope. She made a new knot on the end, climbed on the stool, and reached up to put the knot over the hook. The weight of the clothes dragged down the line. Before I could hold them up, she gave the line an impatient jerk and the knot broke loose from the hook on the other wall.

"You did that on purpose!" I said.

"You're not funny, Paula." She threw the line to the floor and jumped off the stool. "We'll fix this when I get home tonight."

I fixed it when I came home from school. I thought I'd better. If her suits got wrinkled, she might lose it. I just wanted her a *little* sick of me.

It took me an hour to get everything in place. I had to take all the clothes off the line, re-tie the knots, hook them to the wall, straighten the jackets and blouses, and hang them up. I dust-mopped the floor for good measure.

Mom was fine at dinner. Grandma wasn't. Her mouth wrinkles puckered and her gray hair straggled down her ears.

"How come your hair's a mess?" I asked her.

"Because of the baby-faced vice principal."

I didn't get it. Even Mom looked confused.

"The man's totally incompetent." Grandma spit out her words. "He can't even control sophomores in the halls."

"And so?" I asked.

"So they fill up balloons at the water fountains and lean over the second-floor railing and drop them on people coming up the stairs."

The picture of Grandma being soaked by a water balloon was too much for me. I choked on my mouthful of macaroni and dived for the kitchen sink. After I had myself together, I sat down and primly inquired, "Did you catch the kids?"

Grandma ignored me. Mom asked her if she'd like to go to the talent show the PTA was putting on at my school Saturday night. Grandma said attending a school function was the last thing she wanted to do on her weekend.

During dessert, I figured my time had come. I ate three small bites of strawberry ice cream before making the casual remark. "Dad said he might be able to find some scrap lumber."

At the word "Dad," Mom put down her spoon. "What does he need scrap lumber for?"

"To make a partition in the basement so I could sleep down there."

"That might be a good place for you," she said.

I dropped the subject right there. Later I could remind her she told me the basement would be a good place for me.

My plans were going so well I managed to sleep right through Mom's snores. In the morning, I didn't even complain about having no dessert for my lunch. Sukey's whole lunch was dessert.

While half-listening to Karen's questions about whether she should play a piece by Ravel or Mozart for the talent show, I watched Sukey. She took one chocolate cupcake after another out of her lunch sack. She certainly didn't eat healthy food. Anyone would be pale who ate like she did.

"Paul-a! Do you think the audience would like the 'Bolero' best?" Karen had leaned over the aisle and jabbed my arm to get my attention centered on her.

Nick leaned forward from the seat behind me and poked Karen's arm. "Kar-en! It doesn't matter what you play because as soon as you put your paws on the piano, it's nap time."

I giggled. Karen withdrew to her desk to chew on her pieces of string cheese. Mr. Loyal looked up from his lunch.

"Sukey," he said, "I don't know if you've heard that we're having a talent show here Saturday evening. Would you like to be in it?"

"Okay," Sukey said.

Okay? The whole class stared at her.

"What would you like to do?" Mr. Loyal asked.

"I guess I could bring my guitar and play a song."

"That would be a treat for us," Mr. Loyal said. "We're having a rehearsal after school tomorrow. Will you be able to stay for it?"

"I guess so. I think my mom can pick me up after it's over."

Whoa! I wondered if her mom would drive a tan car.

Sukey brought her guitar to school the next morning and all of us kids gathered around her desk to see it. "Open the case," Nick demanded.

Sukey unlatched the case and we all stared at the shiny guitar. "What piece are you going to play?" Karen asked.

"Probably 'Ring-Around-a-Rosy' and the pickle song," Sukey said.

I faded toward my half of the room. "Ring-Around-a-Rosy" and the pickle song? I hoped Sukey didn't bomb.

After school on Thursday, I walked Bitsey down the street by the creek. She tried to pull me into the woods, but I only let her sniff around the bushes lining the road. I wanted to see if the tan car was still parked in the same place.

It was. There was a paper fan over the windshield, the kind used to keep out the sun, and there were curtains on the side windows. I walked slowly past the car, trying to get a quick peek around the fan. I turned about a block up the road, let Bitsy do her job, and walked slowly back past the car again. Not a stir inside.

The next morning, the only empty seat on the bus was the one in front of me. After Sukey settled in it, I tapped her shoulder. "How did the rehearsal go?"

She tilted her head around to say, "All right."

"Did your Mom drive you home?"

"No, she couldn't. Mr. Loyal asked one of the other mothers to drop me at my street."

"That was nice of him. He's—" I cut myself off because Sukey was facing the front of the bus again.

Dad arrived at our house early Saturday morning. As soon as I heard his truck, I slipped quietly out of bed without waking Mom, got dressed, and let him in the back door. He was carrying his hammer, electric saw, and a paper sack of nails.

I stood on tiptoe to give him a kiss on his cheek. "You didn't shave," I told him.

"No, I thought you'd rather have me spend the time on your wall. I'll clean up before I go to work tonight."

I led him down the basement stairs. "Where are you working?"

"The bartender at the tavern has an ulcer and I'm pinch-hitting for him."

"Do you get good tips?" I asked.

"Every once in a while." Dad put his tools on the cement floor and surveyed the basement. "Let's see, you don't want those old washtubs in your room. Or my old workbench. Why don't we move Grandma's trunks and furniture over by the tubs and have your room on the south end. That will give you two windows and a light."

I looked up at the bare bulbs on the ceiling. "How am I going to turn them off and on? The switch is at the top of the stairs."

"I guess you'll have to stand on the stool and unscrew the lights when you want it dark. Later we can get you new sockets with long chains. Okay?"

"Sure." I gave him a shove toward Grandma's piano bench. He carried it to the washtubs. I pushed a trunk across the floor. Mom must have heard the commotion, because just as we finished clearing the space, she came down the stairs.

"What's going on?" The expression on her face was cold and hard. It sank my courage to my feet. My plan to remind her that she'd said the basement was a good place for me sank, too.

Dad stroked his chin, watching her walk toward us.

"What're you doing here?" she asked him.

"I'm putting up a wall for Paula." He reached into the back pocket of his jeans and took out his wallet. "I have fifty bucks for you."

She took the bill from him without looking at it. "You owe me six hundred."

"I know I do. And I'll pay you every bit I can until I'm caught up."

"You jolly well better. You miss one more support payment and you'll be in jail." With that, she turned and went back up the stairs.

"Can she really put you in jail?" I whispered to Dad.

"Don't worry. She won't have to." He put his arm around my shoulders. "Come on. Let's haul in the two-by-fours."

The Pickle Song

Dad used two-by-fours to make the frame for the partition. After he measured and sawed the boards, I handed them to him so he could nail them in place. When we went out to his truck for the plywood, he took one end of the sheets and I took the other. It was tricky walking backward down the basement steps. The plywood sheets were warped, but Dad managed to get them pounded straight.

Next came the cedar shakes. That was the good part. He shingled the wall inside my room and then he shingled the outside. We stood by the washtubs and surveyed the finished job. "Cool!" I said. "Just like a cabin."

"How would you like an eave coming down from the top?" he asked.

"That'd be even better."

Dad nailed a line of two-by fours up next to the ceiling and slanted cedar shakes over them. "Now it looks like the edge of a real roof," I said. "This is so neat."

I pulled the plywood door open and we went inside my room. First I stared happily at the shakes and then scuffed my feet against the stained cement. "Too bad this floor is so ugly."

"A coat of paint would fix it," Dad said. "We'll get a can later."

"How much does it cost? I think I've got eight dollars saved."

Dad was leaning against the new wall and he reached out to ruffle my hair. "For living in a poor family, you're a hard woman with money."

"Well, if I save it, I have it when I need it. Right?"

"Right." He pulled his wallet from his back pocket. "A gallon will cost you about eleven bucks. Here's another three."

I could see the three dollars were all that was left in his wallet so I pushed the money back. "That's okay. I can wait. Grandma gives me two dollars a week to walk her dog after school."

"No, take it," he insisted, shoving the bills my way again. "I'll get more cash tonight. Just be sure you get the kind of paint that goes on cement."

I took the money, Dad gathered up his tools, and we walked out to his truck. "I've agreed to work next weekend, too," he told me as he dumped his stuff in the back. "I'll miss having you, but I'd better catch up on the payments for your mom."

"You'd better," I agreed.

"You made friends with that Sukey yet?"

"I'm trying," I said. "She's going to be in the talent show tonight."

"I think maybe you should be careful not to ask questions when you talk to her. It'd be easy to ask her where she lives or what her parents do, but that might scare her off." Dad leaned down, kissed me goodbye, and climbed in the driver's seat.

As I watched him drive away, I thought he'd given me good advice. I do ask too many questions and I didn't want to scare Sukey off.

On the way back to the house, I checked my watch. Four-thirty and I was starving. Grandma came in the kitchen and frowned at my peanut butter sandwich. "Won't that spoil your dinner?"

"Dinner?" I said. "I haven't had any breakfast or lunch."

"You were making enough noise downstairs."

"I know. Do you want to see my new room? Come on, I'll show you."

Grandma picked her way down the basement steps and carefully eyed the cedar shake wall. "Well, that is kind of cute."

"Come inside. He did this wall, too."

She stopped at the door to examine the knob Dad'd made from a chuck of two-by-four. "There's no lock. Aren't you the girl who's afraid to go in the basement at night?"

"Not if my bed's here. And I can get a bolt for the door later."

Grandma stepped inside. She looked at the wall, the windows, and then the splotched floor.

I hurried to assure her, "Those stains won't show after the floor's painted. Do you like my room?"

"It's a start," she said.

During dinner, I didn't mention my new room or invite Mom downstairs. Instead, I talked about Sukey playing her guitar in the talent show. "That'll be a relief after the screechy orchestra," Mom said.

Casey's in the band. He plays a mean trombone, but I didn't argue with Mom. I asked what she was going to wear.

"My brown suit, I think."

I wore my yellow shirt and clean jeans.

The orchestra opened the talent show. I admit the

violins were screechy. They played three pieces and when they were finished, the members filed off the stage to take seats in the audience. Casey sat behind me. He thumped the back of my chair with his knees when Mr. Edmonds, the school principal, announced Karen Elridge.

She pranced out on the stage in a long white dress, a big white hair ribbon, and black ballet shoes. As soon as she raised her hands over the piano keys, Casey let out a snore. A gray-haired lady on the other side of me hissed at him.

Karen pounded out her dumb "Bolero" for what seemed like an hour. When she finally finished, the parents in the audience clapped politely. We kids smacked our hands because we were glad she was getting off the stage.

A fourth grade ballet dancer was next. And then Sukey!

After her introduction, Sukey came on carrying her guitar and a chair. She placed the chair at the front of the stage and sat down to softly finger her guitar. She was wearing her old jeans and a clean blue turtleneck sweater I hadn't seen before.

It was a while before she looked up at the audience, flipped her dark hair over shoulder, and talked to us. "This is my daddy's guitar." Strum. "My daddy loved Arlo Guthrie's songs." Strum. "Maybe some of you have heard of Woody Guthrie, Arlo's daddy. He traveled around with his guitar until he got sick. With all his traveling, I don't know how he took care of Arlo." Pause. "Maybe he didn't.

"I'm going to sing you a song Arlo wrote called 'Ring-Around-a-Rosy Rag.' "

My worrying about Sukey bombing was for nothing. The ricky-ticky way she played and sang "Touch your nose and blow your toes" had Casey clicking his knuckles on my chair and the rest of us bouncing.

"Come on," Sukey called out. "Touch your noses and blow your toeses."

We all touched our noses and bent down to blow our toes. Even Mom.

Sukey ended the song to a roar of laughter. "Next," she said, "I'm going to sing the pickle song."

The song was about a man who didn't want a pickle. He just wanted to ride his motorcycle. And everyone the man met didn't want a pickle. They wanted to ride their motorcycle. The way Sukey sang it "cycle" rhymed with "pickle."

"Now," Sukey said, "when I call out your name, you tell me what you want."

Sukey sang, "I met a boy named Casey and Casey told me—"

From behind me came Casey's crackly voice, "I don't want a pickle. I just want to ride my motorcycle."

Before I could turn back from craning my neck at

Casey, Sukey sang out, "Paula doesn't have a bike, but she says—"

Panic! Casey thumped my seat. I gulped. Out came my wavering voice, "I don't want a pickle. I just wish I had a motorcycle."

"Good for you," Mom whispered.

"I didn't even know she knew my name," I whispered back.

Sukey strummed out the last of the song, stood up, and gave the audience a little nod. We all beat our hands together.

Mr. Edmonds caught Sukey at the side curtain and turned her around for another bow. Still holding her guitar and chair, Sukey bowed and then bowed again.

The talent show ended with three fifth grade boys and their yo-yos. They sang along with their tricks. They got through Walk the Dog and Around the World. When they came to Rock the Baby, one kid's voice dribbled away on the last "Baby, Baby, Baby" because his yo-yo was tangled in the cradle. Mr. Edmonds thanked the boys anyway and thanked everyone else for coming.

Mom immediately gathered up her purse. I went up the aisle after her, tugging on her jacket. "Mom, wait. Let's congratulate Sukey."

"We will if we see her on the way out."

Sukey was in the front hall holding her guitar case. A lady in a flowered dress stood beside her. While we waded through the kids around Sukey, I took a good look at the lady. She had fluffy blond hair and a friendly smile. She seemed like a regular mom to me.

"You did great," I told Sukey when we reached her.

"Thanks," she said. Off the stage, she was shy again and hardly looked me in the face.

"Those were charming songs, dear," Mom told her before pulling me toward Karen and her mother.

I pulled back. "I'm not going to say I liked Karen's piano playing."

Mom tightened her grip. "Doing a little kindness never hurt anybody."

"Well, it's hurting me," I said, prying her fingers off my arm.

Only parents were around Karen. Mom told Mrs. Elridge that she certainly had a talented daughter. Karen shot me a nervous glance.

"So, you decided on the 'Bolero,' " I said.

"Casey and Nick probably hated it."

It hadn't dawned on me until then that Karen worried about what kids thought of her. I'd assumed she fussed about choosing a piece because she wanted to show off.

While Karen stared sadly at her ballet shoes, I thumbed through my mind for something real to say. "It was a pretty good talent show."

"Everyone liked Sukey," she said.

"Ya," I agreed. "Well, see you Monday."

People were streaming out to the parking lot. As Mom and I walked through the school's front doors, I searched through the crowd for a girl carrying a guitar case and a woman in a flowered dress. "There she is!" I told Mom. "There she is!"

"Who?"

"Sukey and her mother. And they're getting in the *tan* car."

The Hip-Hop Painting

On Monday, after he'd taken roll, Mr. Loyal asked if there were any volunteers for lunch duty. John and Spencer and I raised our hands. Mr. Loyal called on me.

"I've never done it," I said, "and neither has Sukey. Can we do it together?"

"I don't see why not." He turned to Sukey. "Would you like to be on lunch duty for the next two weeks?"

"What would I do?" she asked cautiously.

"You'd help the cooks serve the food and take the trays back to the gym after lunch is over."

"Sometimes the cooks give you two desserts," Nick put in.

"I wouldn't count on that," Mr. Loyal said. "But you'll get your free hot lunch early. I'll expect you to make up any assignments you miss, of course."

Sukey's eyes had swiveled to the side at the words "free hot lunch." I tried to decide if getting a free lunch embarrassed or interested her.

Mr. Loyal was watching her, too. "Shall I put your names down?"

Sukey nodded and he passed the roll sheet to Evelyn, who was office monitor for October.

All through arithmetic, I smiled to myself. As Grandma says, I'd killed two birds with one stone. Sukey would get something else to eat besides cinnamon rolls and I'd have a chance to make friends with her.

We had our hot lunch in an empty classroom while the cooks set up food tables in the hall. The fish sticks were soggy, so I filled up on corn bread. Sukey ate everything on her tray. I didn't talk to her then because the workers from other rooms kept asking her questions about her guitar. Before we'd finished eating, a cook came in to see if we needed more food. The guys all wanted another brownie. I did, too.

"How about you?" the cook asked Sukey.

"Maybe another half orange," she said.

After the guys and I porked down the brownies and Sukey sucked her orange dry, we dumped our trays on the empty cart and put on plastic caps and gloves. One room is let out at a time in our school. The kids pick up trays at the beginning of the line and walk down the tables for the food.

Sukey's job was to pass out tartar sauce for the fish sticks, I was in charge of the brownies, and Kenny, Casey's friend in his sixth grade room, handed out corn bread. Between servings, Kenny imitated a surgeon by holding his arms in the air with the serving knife in one gloved hand. This got a snicker out of the fourth graders.

When we were through with the lunch lines, Sukey and I collected tray carts outside the classrooms and rolled them into the gym. I was careful not to ask her questions. Instead, I told her about my grandma coming to stay because my mom was out of money. I thought this would loosen Sukey up.

It did. She stopped watching the pathway between the buildings and turned her head to listen to me. I went on about my mom snoring and my getting Dad to build me a room in the basement.

I had to quit talking to open the gym doors. Kenny's cart rumbled up behind us. We took turns lifting the trays off the carts and depositing them on the counter inside the kitchen. Kenny finished first, but he took a ball out of the gym's storage box and shot a couple of hoops, which he wasn't supposed to do. Sukey and I walked over to our room.

"I'm going to buy some paint after school. Wanna go to the hardware store with me?" I asked her.

She thought this over with her finger in her mouth. "The hardware store is across the street from the Lake Stevens Post Office, isn't it?"

"Ya, do you have to go there?"

"I usually do after school."

Strange, I'd never seen her anywhere on the road, except to catch the bus. "We have some extra brushes. Do you want to help me paint the floor, too?"

"Okay," she said.

I hadn't expected this to be so easy. Before I opened our classroom door, I nailed down our agreement. "I'll meet you at the gas station right after I walk Grandma's dog."

"Okay," she said again and we went into our room.

Sukey was waiting when I got to the gas station. The natural way for me to start a conversation was to ask her where she lived. I could barely keep the question from coming out of my mouth.

I distracted myself by talking about Mr. Loyal. Sukey didn't listen. She made tracks for the little Lake Stevens Mall like a cat after a squirrel. "I'll come to the hardware store as soon as I finish in the post office," she said.

"No, that's all right. I'll go to the post office with you first."

What could she say?

I followed her right up to the counter. "Is there a general delivery letter for Mrs. Parsons?" she asked the clerk.

She watched him intently as he sorted through the boxes behind the counter. After he turned and told her there was no letter, she kept staring at him as if she couldn't take in his words. Her pale face had gone even paler. I poked her. "Let's go."

She dragged along behind me, kicking gravel as we crossed to the hardware store. "Too bad your letter wasn't there," I said.

She didn't lift her head, just kept watching the toes of her shoes spraying the gravel in circles ahead of her. I wondered if she was too bummed out to paint the floor, but I guess she wasn't. After I bought the paint, she went down the hill with me toward my house.

We met Casey at the corner. He eyed the can I was carrying. "Hip-hop time?"

"No, my dad made me a new room in the basement and I'm covering the stains on the floor."

"You'll need professional help," he decided and swung in beside us.

When we reached my back door, Casey took the basement steps two at a time. "Aw right!" he said, sliding his hands down the shakes. "Good job."

"It looks like a real house," Sukey said. She seemed to be perking up.

"What are you going to call it?" Casey asked me.

"I don't know. I haven't—"

"I'll think of a name," he said. "You got any spray cans?"

"Maybe, on Dad's old workbench. But only do the door. I want the shakes natural."

"Of course." He rummaged around in the cans and bottles while I got two brushes for Sukey and me.

"We'll start on one side and put the paint bucket between us," I told Sukey.

She nodded and we got down on our knees inside the room. We could hear Casey saying, "Ah, here's black. Aaa-nd here's yellow." Then he shut the door and we couldn't hear him anymore.

"What was the yellow for?" Sukey asked.

"That was for our bathroom," I said. "Dad touched up the wall where the hamper banged it."

By the time we'd covered half the floor, the paint smell was getting to me. I yelled at Casey to bring in the stool so I could open one of the windows. He thumped the stool down inside the door. "You realize you interrupted an artist."

"Sorry about that," I said.

He left and Sukey asked, "Is he any good?"

"Ya, his dad has a tattoo studio in Seattle. Casey

inked dragons on all the guys' arms until some mom complained and the principal made him stop it."

Sukey's a good worker and we painted until our bottoms were up against the door. "We're coming out," I hollered.

"Hold on a sec," Casey hollered back.

"His sign better be good," I muttered.

It was. He'd sprayed the whole door with reeling yellow figures. In black letters, he'd written on top of the figures:

STAGGER INN

AND

DROP

"That's great!" I told him "That's so neat."

Sukey looked at me worriedly. "Will your mother be mad?"

"Grandma will. But who cares."

Casey pulled the door open wide. "Don't you think you need something on this side, too?"

"Absolutely." I clapped my hands together. "A dragon to keep the evil spirits away!"

"I'll need a brush for that."

While Casey found a thin brush on the workbench, I finished the last bit of floor. He took the bucket away from me. "I'll use the brown for the dragon."

Sukey and I stood back and watched him paint a huge dragon standing on its hind feet and blowing smoke out of its nose. "You got any red?" he asked.

"Maybe I have a red marker on my desk."

"Get it," he ordered.

With the red pen, he added fire to the smoke.

"That is absolutely fantastic," I said.

Sukey shook her head in amazement.

Casey took up the black spray can and wrote the letters K.C. in the top corner, just as he had on the front of the door.

"What does K.C. mean?" Sukey asked. "Oh! Oh, *Casey!*"

"That's my signature," he told her.

I walked them out to my front porch. "Maybe you guys can come tomorrow and help me carry my bed and desk down."

"That's work," Casey said. "You two can do it."

"I'll come after I go to the post office," Sukey promised.

At dinner I was still so excited about my painted door and floor that I invited Mom and Grandma down to see it.

Grandma's neck jerked back when she saw the door. "What is that mess?"

"That's a hip-hop painting," I said.

"It looks like scribbling to me."

Mom put her hand on Grandma's arm. "You know, Mother, we used to call it graffiti."

I opened the door to show them the dragon.

"Who did that? Casey?" Mom asked.

"Yes, isn't he good?"

Grandma couldn't say he wasn't. She said, "A 'fraidy cat like you will last about one hour in a dark basement with a dragon."

"We'll see," I said.

Hocking Grandma's Bracelet

Sukey's promise was good. She arrived at my house as I was bringing Bitsey in from her walk. I took Sukey into my bedroom and we yanked the covers off my bed. She carried my rocker downstairs while I carried my blankets.

"Now the mattress and springs," I said as we trudged back up the steps. "Those are going to be heavy."

They were. It was worse than when Dad and I brought in the plywood because Sukey isn't as strong as he is. We managed, though. And we got the bed apart and set up downstairs.

We pulled the drawers out of my desk and dresser and took those next. We almost didn't make it with the empty dresser. I was going backward and lost my grip on the legs. If Sukey hadn't held on, the dresser would have slipped down the stairs and smashed me into the cement.

"Let's take a break," I said. "My arms are giving out."

Up in the kitchen, I stuffed two glasses with ice and poured pineapple juice over the top. From the way Sukey ate oranges, I thought she'd like pineapple. She did.

"This is really good," she said.

"Cold, too. Did you get the letter you wanted today?"

"No. It wasn't there."

I didn't want her depressed again, so I said quickly, "I've never seen you on the road. How do you get to the post office?"

"I take a shortcut and come around the back of the mall."

"Oh."

We were sitting on the mattress together. I leaned on my elbow and stared at Casey's dragon. "I wish I had the money to buy a bolt for that door. Grandma says I'll be scared in the dark basement all alone."

"Will you?"

"Probably, but I wouldn't be if I had a lock."

"How much does a bolt cost?"

"I don't know. Maybe three dollars and I've got exactly twenty-two cents. Grandma gives me money for walking her mutt, but she'd never give me an advance."

Sukey sipped her drink slowly. She seemed to be going over something in her mind. I hoped she didn't think I wanted to borrow money from her. I was about to set her straight when she said, "Have you got anything made out of gold? Jewelry? A ring or a bracelet?"

"I have a bracelet my other grandma gave me before she died, but it's old. It belonged to her mother."

"If it's real gold," Sukey said, "you can hock it for money."

"What's hocking? I don't know anything about hocking things."

Sukey shrugged. "It's easy. You take your bracelet to a pawnshop and the owner runs a test to be sure it's real and then he gives you money and a ticket. You can just keep the money and forget the bracelet. Or when you get more money, you can turn in your ticket and get your bracelet back."

"But what if the owner sells the bracelet?"

"He will if you don't pick it up in time. Mom and

I are probably going to the pawnshop tomorrow. I'll take your bracelet if you want me to."

"I don't know." I placed my glass carefully on the floor while I thought. "What if I don't get it back? The thing is, it belonged to my dad's grandmother."

Sukey drained the last of the pineapple juice into her mouth. "Whatever. Do what you want. You can finish the moving, can't you? I have to go."

I bounced off the mattress. "Wait, wait. First help me put the springs and mattress on the frame. I can't do that alone."

Sukey helped me put the bed together and then she left, leaving me mad at myself. I should have been nicer when she offered to hock the bracelet. For scaring her away, I had to put the drawers in my dresser and desk by myself. And pack down all my clothes.

They were still piled on the floor when I went to bed. Mom came into the basement to kiss me good night. "You sure you'll be all right here?"

"Of course," I said.

"Do you want me to leave the flashlight with you in case you have to go to the bathroom in the night?"

I had the sense to say yes. After she was gone, I turned on the flashlight and stood on my bed to turn off the ceiling light. The bare bulb was hot and every time I tried to unscrew it, my fingers burned. By licking my fingers and giving the bulb quick twists, I finally got it off. I was so tired and frustrated by then I collapsed onto my bed, pulled up my covers, and fell asleep.

Someone was in my room. It was pitch black and I couldn't see him, but I could hear him. He made a soft shuffling sound as he moved closer and closer to my bed. I tried to scream, but nothing came out of my mouth.

He shuffled closer and closer. I managed to squeak, "Mama!" before gloved fingers clutched my throat. Scratch him, scratch him, I thought, but my arms wouldn't move. The gloved fingers tightened. I gagged—

And woke up. My heart was racing. Sweat covered my chest. I turned my head to look at the flashlight on the brass trunk beside my bed. Only a weak yellow glimmer shined from it.

I lay in bed thinking that I had to get up and go to the bathroom. I had to stand on the bed and try to screw the light bulb on or make my way upstairs in the faint beam of the flashlight. I wouldn't be able to go back to sleep unless I did.

I was about to push off my blankets when a muffled thump came from the other side of the basement. I froze with my eyes opened wide. No more sounds. I listened, not moving a muscle. What would make that thump in the night? A mouse jumping off the workbench?

I had to go to the bathroom, but I couldn't get up. I couldn't make myself get up and go out in the dark basement. I lay there a long, long time. Still listening.

Light was seeping through the high windows by the time I fell asleep again and dreamed I was hunting for the girls' rest room. I found one on the primary side of the school, but when I went inside, the toilets had flooded the floor.

"Well, you're looking poorly this morning," Grandma said, picking up her coffee cup from the breakfast table. "Didn't you sleep?"

"No!" I snapped at her. "And, Mom, I think we have mice."

"You do? Have you seen any droppings?"

"I didn't look. I heard some animal thumping around in the basement, though."

Grandma pursed her lips. "Perseverance toward a goal is commendable. But willfulness—"

Mom sighed. "Please, Mother, not this morning. Paula, I'll put a mousetrap down there tonight."

Mom got up to go to work. I went downstairs. Grandma was left at the table by herself.

After I put on my jacket, I stood in front of my dresser trying to make a decision. Should I or shouldn't I? My hand made the decision for me. It opened the top drawer and lifted the gold bracelet out of my jewelry box.

Sukey must have been sorry she said anything to me about pawnshops. Maybe she thought she'd given away too much about herself. Maybe she thought I'd think that's where she went when she needed money. And that's what I did think.

If she and her mom were living in a car, how else could they get money? But then again, how much stuff can you keep in a car to hock?

I was going over these things in my mind while we were eating lunch. She'd chosen a seat away from me again. I guess she thought that would hold me off, but she wasn't on to my willfulness the way Grandma was. I waited.

I waited until we were alone, pushing the carts with dirty trays. I stopped at the gym doors and before I opened them, I pulled the bracelet from a pocket in my jeans. "Here," I said. "Can you hock this for me today?"

She backed away a bit. "Are you sure? Are you sure you won't get in trouble?"

"Who's going to know? You won't tell, will you?"

She took the bracelet and stuffed it in her jeans pocket. "No. I don't tell things."

I giggled. "I believe that."

And then she had to giggle, too.

I felt great about the whole transaction right up until I was in bed that night. Mom had put a mousetrap under Dad's old workbench and I was figuring on a good night's rest. I went right off to sleep and was into my first dream when a loud bang sat me straight up.

It's a car backfiring, I told myself. Now, take it easy, it's just a car. I couldn't make myself stop trembling. I couldn't see a thing in my room. The weak flashlight wasn't going to help me much and I was afraid my bed would squeak if I tried to stand on it to screw on the light.

I must have shaken for five minutes before the mousetrap came up in my head. You idiot, I told myself and flopped down on my pillow.

I was drifting off to another dream when my eyes popped opened again. I had given Sukey the bracelet to get a bolt for my door. But how was I going to put a lock on the door without my mother finding out? And she would ask, "Where did you get the money for that bolt?" She knew I'd spent my savings on paint.

I twisted and turned on my bed, yelling into my mind, You idiot, you idiot, you double idiot!

I'd given up Grandma Tomlin's bracelet for nothing. And it was a pretty bracelet, too, with swirls of flowers carved in the gold. And for nothing. How was I going to get it back?

Trapped

Sukey sat down beside me on the bus. "Here's your money," she said, slipping it into my hand.

I looked down at the three ten-dollar bills. "That much?"

"It's a lot, isn't it? The pawnshop pays by the ounce and your bracelet was heavy. Lucky you!"

I was so bummed out I couldn't return her furry-toothed smile. It was the end of October and raining. Probably too cold and wet for her to wash in the creek.

"Oh! I almost forgot." Sukey dug into her pants

pocket. "And here's your ticket. It'll cost you thirty-six seventy-five to get your bracelet back."

That made me even sicker. "The interest comes to *six dollars* and seventy-five cents?"

"No, you have to pay a setup fee. The setup fee is five dollars."

"Oh." I'd never heard about a setup fee.

The bus pulled into the schoolyard before we could talk anymore. It was a good thing, too. I wanted to ask her when the pawnshop would put Grandma Tomlin's bracelet up for sale. But if I started in on those questions, Sukey'd know I wished she hadn't done me any favors.

Karen saw us come into the classroom together. As soon as I was in my seat, she leaned across the aisle. "I can't believe you like Sukey Parsons."

"Get out of my face."

She shrank away and I didn't care. It was a relief to take my misery out on her.

On the school bus going home, Sukey sat down with me again. "Are you buying your lock today?"

"I have to walk the dog first."

"I'll meet you at the gas station in a half hour, okay?"

I just nodded. I was busy adding up numbers in my mind. I'd been doing it all day. I was still adding them when I walked Bitsey through the woods.

At two dollars a week it would take four weeks to get the extra six seventy-five. If the bolt cost four dollars, that would be another two weeks. I could forget the bolt, but how would I explain that to Sukey, and anyway, I didn't think I could stand nightmares for a month.

Somewhere I'd gotten the idea that pawnshops would hold items for thirty days. But maybe that was the dry cleaners that held clothes for thirty days. I could call the pawnshop and find out how long before they'd sell the bracelet, but I knew I was too chicken to do that.

Chicken, chicken, chicken, I mumbled to myself, yanking on Bitsey's leash. Chicken, chicken, chicken, I mumbled all the way home. Being chicken of the dark was the beginning of all my trouble.

This time the clerk at the post office whipped out a letter from under the counter when Sukey asked for mail. "Here you are, young lady," he said. "I thought you'd be in again today."

Sukey took the letter, backed out of the way for the next customer, and ripped the envelope apart.

"Are you supposed to open your mom's mail?"

"It doesn't matter." She stared at the money that had been folded inside. "Gee, only twenty dollars."

I waited while she skimmed through the pages of the letter and then stuffed everything back in the torn envelope. "Well, anyway, he's working."

"Who's working?" I asked as she headed for the door.

"Who's working?" I repeated, going after her.

We were outside the post office before she pulled out of her thoughts to answer me. "My dad. He's picking vegetables."

"In October?"

"In California. He'll work in the fields until he gets a job in a restaurant."

A whole bunch more questions about her and her dad flooded my mind, but I didn't ask them. I lifted the hood of my jacket over my head so the rain wouldn't soak my hair. Sukey didn't have a hood on her jacket. "Let's run," I suggested.

I beat her to the hardware store. It took a while before we found the aisle with door locks. The cheapest one I saw was a slot and chain for three ninety-five. Just what I thought I'd have to pay.

"Here's one for a dollar ninety-five." Sukey pointed to a bolt in a hard plastic wrap.

"Let me see that." I nudged her out of the way to check the price tab above the hook holding the packages. Sure enough, $1.95. If I'd waited until after Grandma paid me on Sunday, I could have had my door locked without hocking the bracelet.

Shaking my head with disgust, I jerked the bolt off the hook.

"Don't you like that one?" Sukey asked anxiously. "Don't get it just because I found it."

"I'm not," I said.

We went up to the counter and I paid the clerk.

As we walked down the hill toward the Machias Road, Sukey said, "You have lots of money left."

"Much good it does me. I don't have enough to get my bracelet out of the pawnshop."

"You could just spend the money and get another bracelet someday."

"Not one like my grandma's, I couldn't."

"Do you wish I hadn't taken it to the pawnshop?" Her voice was growing fainter and fainter.

I turned to peek at her through the front of my hood. "It isn't that. If I'd waited until after next Sunday, I would have been able to buy a bolt with the money from walking the dog."

Sukey bowed her head. She was kicking gravel again.

"Hey, it isn't your fault. You were just trying to help me. It's all my fault. I couldn't wait because I get nightmares sleeping in the basement alone. Our house is old and creaky and we have mice."

Sukey's head was still down so I hurried on. "Every morning I bring a mouse up in the trap Mom sets. This morning it was a little baby one. Grandma said there's probably a nest of them, but I can't find it. And every night when the trap snaps, it scares me. And I'm scared anyway. I keep dreaming someone's coming closer and closer to my bed."

"I know about nightmares," Sukey said flatly. I bet she did.

She didn't want to come to my house. She left me at the Machias Road. I walked slowly home, turning every few steps to see where she was going until the trees blotted out my vision. While I was watching, she never crossed the street to where the tan car was parked.

That night, when Grandma came home from teaching school, she was loaded with packages.

"What have you got?" I asked her.

"Nothing for you to know about until after dinner." She dumped the packages on the couch.

I ignored them. I didn't really care what she had.

All through dinner, Grandma shot glances my way with that "I know something you don't know" look on her face. I moved to the side of my chair where I could see only Mom.

During dessert, Grandma said, "Have we got a hammer?"

What did she mean, "we"? This wasn't her house.

"I think so," Mom told her. "It should be on the wall behind the workbench in the basement."

Grandma smiled that sneaky smile again. Her old teeth were as yellow as Sukey's.

"Well," she said, folding her napkin and placing it beside her plate. "Let's all go downstairs. Everyone carry a package."

It hit me then that Grandma was really up to something. I obediently went into the living room, picked up two of the soft, floppy packages, and trotted down to the basement to wait for Grandma and Mom. Mom came first and then Grandma came, holding on to the railing with one hand and carrying a long skinny package in the other.

"Get the hammer, Paula," she ordered.

I got the hammer and we went into my room. "That door swings the wrong way," Grandma said. "It could smack you in the face. You need a latch."

Tell me about it, I said to myself.

She sat down in my rocker and unwrapped the long package while Mom and I watched. Inside the paper were metal rods. "What are those for?" I wanted to know.

"For your windows, silly goose."

"Oh." I was beginning to get it. I brought in the stool, climbed on it, and pounded nails through the holes in the metal brackets Grandma handed me. As I finished each one, Grandma passed up a rod to slip in the brackets.

"Now for the surprise!" She opened one of the floppy packages on my bed where I'd dumped it. Inside were four curtains, two for each window. They were striped red, brown, and cream.

"Oh, those are pretty," I told her.

"You did a lovely job on them, Mother," Mom added.

"Did you make 'em?" I asked.

"Certainly," Grandma said. "I'm a Home Ec teacher, remember?"

"They'll look neat on my windows."

And they did!

Next came a cream bedspread trimmed in the stripes and a silky red cushion for my rocker. There was a wide package left. "What's in that one?" I asked.

"You'll see. Bring in my old piano bench."

I lugged it in, shoved it against the wall by the door, and Grandma placed two striped pillows on it. Fantastic! I gave her a kiss. Right on her old puckery mouth, I planted the kiss.

For a second her eyes watered and I thought she might cry. But she pulled back her shoulders and spoke primly. "Now this place looks more like a girl's room."

Before I went to sleep, and just before I unscrewed the light bulb with the end of my sweater sleeve pulled over my hand, I said, "Good night, pretty room."

Then I got under my covers in the dark to wait for the burglar who'd choke me to death.

The Dumpster

I invited Sukey down to see my room. She liked the red cushion on the rocker best. "It's silk, isn't it?" she asked, running her fingers over the material.

"I think so. Grandma warned me not to spill anything on it because it can't be washed."

Sukey sat on the cushion and rocked. I lay on my bed and surveyed the room. "The only thing left," I said, "is to paint those concrete walls white."

"Why white?" Sukey asked. "Maybe you should use a color that matches the curtains."

"No, white. Because if I paint them white, Casey will want to draw on the one with no windows. Wait a minute. I guess cream would do."

Sukey rocked back and forth while she squinted at the wall. "I hope he draws instead of sprays. I like his drawing better than his hip-hop painting."

"Me, too." I slid off the new spread. "There's an after-school movie on. Let's watch it."

We were still watching the movie when Grandma came home from work. Bitsey danced around her, yapping so loudly we couldn't hear the TV. I managed to introduce Sukey. Grandma was smiling when she said hello, but I noticed she was taking a good look into Sukey's face.

After Sukey left, Grandma said, "That girl's eyes are strange. Is she part Oriental?"

"I don't know."

"Have you seen her mother?"

"Yes, I've seen her mother and she looks like any other mother."

Grandma shook her head. "I'm sure that girl is of a mixed race."

"Oh, Grandma, nobody cares about that stuff anymore. You're so old-fashioned."

That probably hurt her feelings because she scooped up Bitsey and marched into her room and stayed there until Mom came home.

I was helping Mom get dinner when Mr. Willmore knocked on our back door. Mom let him in. "I'm sorry to bother you," he said, "but I need to ask a favor."

A worried look came over Mom's face. "Is Marleen all right?"

Marleen is Mr. Willmore's wife. She'd been staying in bed because she was in danger of having a miscarriage.

"She's fine now," he said. "I took her to the doctor today and he said she could have the baby any time."

Mom counted on her fingers. "It will still be premature."

"A bit," Mr. Willmore agreed. "But Marleen's almost eight months along and the doctor thinks the baby will be strong enough now."

"I'm sure it will be," Mom said. "How can I help you?"

"I have to be at a sales convention in Portland next week. If the baby isn't born by then, will you look in on Marleen and take her to the hospital if her contractions start?"

"Certainly. She can call me any time at work and I'll check in on her every evening."

Mr. Willmore put his hand on the door. "I appreciate that. And if there's an emergency, I can be back in four hours."

"She'll be fine. She'll be fine. We'll take care of her."

Mr. Willmore gave a nod to both Mom and me and went out the door.

"Is it really safe for Mrs. Willmore to have the baby now?" I asked Mom.

"I hope so. And I hope it doesn't come on my watch."

"Me, too." I was imagining boiling towels and a screaming Mrs. Willmore. "Do you know how to cut the cord?"

Mom laughed. "You've been watching too many Westerns on TV. We'll get her to the hospital for that."

The phone rang then. Mom went into the living room to answer it. I knew it was Dad by the way she held the receiver out to me as if it were poisoned.

"Hello, Daddy," I said.

"Hello, honey," he said. "I'll miss having you this weekend, but I've got good news. The mill's starting up full-time and that will put you and me on schedule in two weeks."

"That's good."

"And you can tell your mother I've got a check for her."

I turned to Mom. "Dad's got a check for you."

Her eyes narrowed. "How big?"

I put the phone back up to my mouth. "How big is the check?"

"Five hundred dollars," he said.

"Five hundred dollars," I told Mom.

Her eyes widened.

"Mom's glad," I said.

"I thought she would be. How're you getting along with that homeless girl?"

"Good. Sukey and I are friends now."

"Well, have fun with her and I'll pick you up in two weeks. Same time, same place."

"I'll be ready. I love you, Daddy."

"I love you, too, honey."

We both hung up.

All that evening, I wished I'd asked him to send me money. He might have, no questions asked. Mom would have plenty of questions, though. She always managed to stick around when he was on the phone.

I thought and thought about ways to earn money to get the bracelet out of hock. The best I could come up with was to wait until Mom got Dad's check and then ask her if she had an extra job for me. That plan crumbled on Thursday after his letter arrived.

I handed it to her when she came in the house. She snatched the envelope from me and ripped it open as fast as Sukey'd ripped hers. "I can *finally* pay some bills," she sighed and sat right down at her desk.

Grandma and I were left to get dinner. Grandma's a good cook but she uses about a hundred bowls and pans and expects me to wash them. Mom was in a cheerful mood when we called her to the table. "Do you have something you'd like me to do so I can earn money?" I asked, politely passing her the platter of baked chicken.

Grandma looked up from dishing salad onto her plate. "Two dollars a week is plenty for an eleven-year-old girl. You're supposed to do your part around the house."

And that was that.

At school, I must not have been talking much, because Sukey asked me, "Are you still worrying about your bracelet?"

I pushed the lunch cart a few yards along the cement walkway before I answered. "Well, I was wondering how long before the pawnshop will sell it."

Sukey frowned. "I don't know. We never get anything back. I know they keep adding interest. Some woman was in there when we were and she was arguing about her bill."

"Great."

Sukey was quiet all the way to the gym and while we stacked trays on the kitchen counter. She was thinking, I knew, because I could almost hear the gears grinding in her head as she debated with herself. She must have decided to risk letting me in on more of her life, because on the way to our classroom, she asked, "Do you ever buy lunch?"

"Sometimes," I said, "when Mom has the money and there's something special on the menu."

"Next week our lunch duty's over. Couldn't you ask her for lunch money and then save the dollar?"

"I'd starve," I said.

Sukey waited until Kenny'd passed us in the hall. "You don't need to. You can always get food out of a Dumpster."

"A Dumpster!" I yelled.

Sukey jerked her head sideways to check down the hall. It was empty. "Dumpsters are all right if you pick food wrapped in plastic."

"Hmmm," I said. "I never thought of doing that."

"Only if you want to."

I faced her at our classroom door. "I have to. I don't know any other way to get more money."

Before we went inside, we agreed to meet Sunday at five o'clock in Lake Stevens. Sukey said the bakery dumped their old goods after they closed. The bakers made a fresh batch early Monday morning.

I didn't ask Sukey how she knew so much about the bakery. I guessed she explored back alleys. I knew Casey did. Not me. When it's dark outside, I stay inside.

Sunday afternoon Grandma gave me my pay for walking Bitsey. I announced to her and Mom that I was going to the hardware store to buy a lock for my door. It usually takes me twenty minutes to get to Lake Stevens, but I left our house at four-thirty.

Instead of going by the gas station, I walked down the street toward the tan car. I slowed my steps as I approached it, listening and watching for Sukey to come out. There was no sound and no Sukey.

I crossed the street in slow motion, keeping the car in sight from the corner of my eye. Still no Sukey. I waited at the path to the shortcut as long as I dared, staring at the tan car. The only thing I saw was a pickup truck driving by with two dogs yapping in the back.

Sukey was leaning against the telephone pole in front of the bakery when I got there. "What took you so long?"she asked.

"Terminally slow, I guess."

She grinned. She was in a better mood than I was. And trickier, too. She must have started out fifteen minutes early.

We hung around the bakery until we saw the owners lock up and take off in their car. I thought the Dumpster in back might be smelly. It wasn't. It was full of cartons, sacks, a couple of squashed cakes, and packages of hamburger buns, cinnamon rolls, and doughnuts.

Sukey chose doughnuts and I took cinnamon rolls.

I kept them under my jacket going home and shoved them under my bed when I got there. Before I went to sleep, I put the bolt on my door. I thought it would take care of my nightmares, but the clack of the mousetrap still sat me straight up in bed. That mother mouse must have had a dozen hungry babies.

Monday morning, Sukey climbed on the bus and took the seat beside me. "Did it work?"

"Yup, I told her we were having pizza and she gave me the money. I had to use an old nail sack for three cinnamon rolls. I can't eat a whole dozen."

Sukey giggled and giggled again when I made a face at her across the room at lunchtime. We both were taking our food out of wrinkled sacks. I started in on my first cinnamon roll. It tasted funny, but I got it down without anything to drink. The second one tasted worse.

After the first bite, I turned the roll over. There were curls of green mold in the folds of dough. Oh, ugh! I spit my mouthful on a sheet of paper, stuffed the paper and the roll into the nail sack, and sat at my desk shuddering until lunchtime was over.

Confessions

I felt icky all day, and after I went to bed that night, I told myself if Sukey asked me to go to the Dumpster again, I'd say my mom wouldn't pay for more lunches. But that decision left me with my miserable questions. Did interest go up by day or month? How long would the pawnshop owner wait before he sold the bracelet? Another week?

About midnight, the phone rang and I heard Mom's footsteps pattering to the living room. Now what? I'd forgotten about Mrs. Willmore until I rolled over and saw lights from next door filtering through my curtained windows.

I dressed by the dim flashlight and caught Mom just as she opened the front door. "Oh, you're up," she said. "I didn't want to wake Grandma. Come on, you can help me get Marleen in the car."

I followed Mom out the door and into the rain. Mrs. Willmore was waiting on her front porch. Mom put an arm around her and I took the baby's blanket and Mrs. Willmore's suitcase. It was a slow walk to our garage.

In the driveway, Mrs. Willmore bent over, gasping. Mom kept encouraging her. "Come on, Marleen. Come on. We have to get you to the hospital."

I not only wanted her to get to the hospital. I wanted out of the rain. It was pouring down my neck. "Give me the keys," I said to Mom. "This blanket's getting soaked."

When I had the suitcase and blanket stashed, I pulled up my hood and returned to help Mom with Mrs Willmore. After much coaxing and nudging, we got her in the front seat. Mom put the car in gear, zoomed out of the garage, and tore down the road.

All the way to the hospital, Mrs. Willmore moaned, "Hurry, hurry! You better hurry!" And Mom looked wildly from one side of the freeway to the other. "Where are the police when you need them?"

We were met at the emergency entrance by two

attendants with a wheelchair. They hurried Mrs. Willmore to an elevator while Mom was escorted to the office to fill out papers. When she had that finished, we went in the waiting room to wait. "Did you call Mr. Willmore?" I asked.

"Yes, I did that at the house." Mom picked up a magazine from the table.

I chose one, too. Every time I saw a baby born on TV, the family had to sit around for hours. I guess that's not real life, either, because I'd barely read one page when a nurse came into the room with a mask hanging around her neck. "The Willmore baby?" she asked.

Mom jumped up, introduced herself as a neighbor, and explained that Mr. Willmore was on his way from Portland. The nurse told us the girl-baby weighed five pounds eight ounces and was doing fine. Mrs. Willmore was doing fine, too, and we could see her the next day during visiting hours.

I was disappointed. I'd never seen a newborn baby. "They were probably cleaning her up," Mom explained.

I wasn't sure why the baby needed to be cleaned up. Was she bloody? I was too tired to ask, though, and fell asleep on the ride to our house.

Mom took me with her to visit Mrs. Willmore when she came home on Friday. The baby was in a bassinet beside Mrs. Willmore's chair in the living room. Mr. Willmore, who's short and pudgy instead of tall and handsome like my dad, had me sit on the couch. He proudly lifted up the baby and brought it over to put in my lap.

I held the baby with one hand, and with the other I peeled back the blanket from its face. It was an ugly, tiny thing. Blotchy red with a deep frown over its nose.

"Oh, she's sweet," Mom said.

What?

With its eyes scrunched shut, the baby turned its bald head toward my chest. "She's hungry," Mr. Willmore announced.

I shoved it into his hands and he took it to Mrs. Willmore. She unbuttoned her blouse, pulled down the flap of her bra, and stuck the baby against her breast. Mr. Willmore beamed at his beak-nosed wife.

"I hope the kid doesn't grow up to look like her parents," I told Mom on the way home.

"She probably will," Mom said.

Before I kissed her good night, I confessed, "You know the flashlight you lent me? I left it on too long and the batteries wore down."

"It can happen," Mom said. "I'll buy new batteries tomorrow."

That was so easy I wasn't even scared feeling my way down the basement stairs and teetering on my bed to screw on the light. When I had my pajamas on, I screwed off the light and lay down in my bed, wishing it would be easy to confess about Grandma Tomlin's bracelet. I tried a scene in my head where I told Mom everything, except the Dumpster part.

Even though Mom was feeling generous since Dad'd sent the check, I didn't imagine she'd pay the pawn ticket without punishing me. She'd say that I didn't seem to be able to handle money. Grandma would put in that she had to work for the money she paid out. And I wouldn't say that so did I. Mom would say maybe I shouldn't play with Sukey anymore. And Grandma would say I was letting Sukey lead me around by my nose. On and on.

I gave up the scene with Mom and tried to think about telling Dad. The bad part was that his mother had given me the bracelet. I remembered she'd said in front of him, "Now be careful not to lose this, Paula. It can never be replaced."

By the next morning when Dad came to pick me up, I was so depressed, I could hardly smile at him. I was even more depressed when I read the dinner menu at Rotten Ralph's. The hot dog relish reminded me of green mold.

"Things not going so good at home?" Dad asked.

"They're okay. Grandma's a pain, but Mom's better since you sent her the check."

Dad leaned across the table to look into my eyes. "What's eating at you then?"

So I spilled the whole thing. Being scared of the

dark, having nightmares, wishing for a bolt for the door, hocking the bracelet, climbing in the Dumpster.

At the end of my story, *Dad* was depressed. He blamed everything on himself. "I shouldn't have built such a flimsy door. At least I should have gotten you a lock."

"Oh, no! You built me a great room. It's just that I'm chicken."

He shook his head and smiled me a sad smile. "No, you're not. You're the same as any other kid. When my mom made me take out the garbage after dinner, I used to race out of our house to the garbage can and race back in to escape the monsters in the dark.

"We'll get you some sockets with long chains tomorrow and I'll put them in when I take you home. At least you'll be able to turn the lights on and off in the basement."

"That'd be nice." And then I added in a little voice, "But how am I going to get the bracelet back?"

"Have you got the ticket with you?"

"Sure. I don't want Mom or Grandma to find it."

"Give it to me."

I dug into my jeans pocket and handed the ticket to him. He read the small print quickly before he stuffed it in his wallet. "Our usual for dessert?" he asked. I nodded and he ordered the sundaes at the counter.

While I twirled strings of fudge against the dish so it wouldn't drip down my chin, I told Dad that I'd give him the thirty-five dollars I had hidden under my mattress.

"No, you keep that," he said. "I'll take care of the ticket."

"But it's almost enough to get the bracelet out. And thirty of it isn't really mine."

"Consider it yours now," he said. "We don't want you hanging out in Dumpsters."

"Never again," I told him and gulped down the rest of my sundae without tasting it. The bracelet was coming back. The bracelet was safe. I had thirty-five dollars. Thirty-five dollars!

As I wiped my mouth with a paper napkin, I saw Leslie, the bevel sawyer, come in the front door. I ducked my head, hoping she wouldn't see us. I didn't need her barging in on my time with Dad.

"Hello, Carter. Hi, Paula."

"Oh, hi, Leslie," I mumbled.

She reached out with her good hand and pulled one of Dad's black curls away from his forehead. She was smiling at him as if he were the chocolate fudge sundae. My dad has that effect on women. He could be a movie star, except for his broken nose. It got busted in a fight, he says. "In a tavern brawl," Mom always adds.

"Sit down, Leslie," Dad said, moving over.

She tossed her ripped leather jacket over the corner of the booth and sat down, still smiling. I wouldn't smile so much if my front tooth were chipped.

Dad asked her if she was going to have dinner.

She took a quick glance at our empty ice cream dishes. "I'll get some coffee."

With her coffee, she settled back in the booth next to Dad. He passed her the bowl of paper packets. "Sugar for the lady?"

Some lady. Her short yellow hair sprang out from the sides of her moon-shaped face. Her bra showed under the thin T-shirt that drooped over her old jeans. And there were cedar stains on her arms.

But I don't think she even cared how she looked. She just sipped her hot coffee and beamed at Dad.

"Well, Paula," Dad said. "What do you think we should do tonight?"

That made me feel better. Maybe he wasn't going to invite her along. I said, "Let's see a movie."

Leslie stood up when we did. I hoped it was only to let Dad by, but she grabbed her leather jacket off the corner of the booth. Dad helped her put it on and all three of us went out the door and walked over to the Arlington theater.

During the first half of the movie, I tried to figure out why Dad put up with her. I decided it must be because she treated him as if he were a big deal and never criticized him like Mom did. When the sexy part came on the screen, I saw Leslie sneak her hand onto Dad's thigh. The stumpy fingers made her hand look like a crouching spider and I wanted to smash it flat.

Tears for Sukey

Dad tied my last red ribbon to the chain hanging from one of the new light sockets. "Now," he said, turning the light on and off by yanking the ribbon, "you can switch them on at the head of the stairs before you come down at night. And pull the one off in your room when you're ready to go to sleep."

"Maybe I'll pull the basement lights off, too," I told him. "Mom might not want me to leave them on all night. She moans about the electric bill."

"I bet she does." He fished in his pocket for his wallet. "Here. Give her this check. It makes us even."

I took the check and followed him up the basement stairs. He hesitated at the outside door to listen to the sounds coming from the kitchen. "She got a boyfriend?"

"I don't think so." I listened, too. A man's voice rumbled through the wall. "Maybe she has, but he's news to me."

Dad lifted one eyebrow toward the kitchen and then grabbed me to hug me goodbye. "See you in two weeks, honey. And I'm sorry about not getting you a real door that locked."

"That's okay. I'm loaded with money now."

He patted my head and took off. I went in the kitchen to check out the man.

He was standing by the sink with a drink in his hand. Mom was beside him with one in hers. This was also news. I thought Mom disapproved of drinking.

She looked startled when she saw me. "Oh, Paula. Ned, this is my daughter, Paula."

He held out his hand to me. "Glad to meet you, little lady."

His hand was as soft as Grandma's. He was taller than Mom, but skinnier. Much skinnier. And his Adam's apple bobbed in his neck when he talked. "You've got your mother's big brown eyes."

"My mother's eyes are gray," I said.

He peered at Mom. "Oh, so they are. I guess I just noticed how big they were."

Mom laughed nervously.

I gave her Dad's check.

She took a quick glance at the face of it before she placed it upside down on the counter. Ned didn't say anything. Mom swirled the drink in her glass.

I was getting the feeling she'd like me out of there. "Guess I'll go see what Grandma's doing."

Grandma was reading a book. "Who's that guy?" I asked her.

She closed her book and placed it on the table by the couch. "He's a tool salesman."

"He works in the hardware store with Mom? I've never seen him there."

"He doesn't work there," Grandma said. "He sells tools to the store. Mostly chain saws, from what I can gather."

I plopped down on the couch with her. "He looks too puny to start up a chain saw."

"He is a scrawny thing."

Grandma told the same thing to Mom after Ned left.

I added my puny bit.

This made Mom mad. "Well, you two, I don't need another big tomcat."

That shut us up. I tried to kiss Mom good night.

She barely turned her head to take my peck. I wanted to say I was sorry we put down her boyfriend, but I didn't.

I left for my room, switching off lights as I went through the basement. After I got in bed, I pulled the red ribbon that dangled above my head. The pitch black didn't even bother me. I fell asleep picturing my rescued bracelet and all the things I could buy with thirty-five dollars.

The next morning, I was set to tell Sukey my news about Dad taking the pawn ticket, but she wasn't on the bus. She wasn't at school either. All through math I thought about her, wondering where she was, wondering if she'd gotten sick.

After school, I walked Bitsey through the woods by the creek. The rain had stopped, but the fallen leaves were slippery under my feet. I didn't see any sign of Sukey having been near the creek. No plastic wrappings from the Dumpster. Nothing.

I had changed direction to go up by the tan car and was tugging Bitsey's leash toward the road when I spotted Sukey. She was crouched under a tree at the edge of the woods. She didn't move as I came close.

"Hi," I said. "You sick?"

She slowly lifted her head from her knees. There were dark shadows around her pale mouth and under her sad eyes.

"What's the matter?" I asked. "You weren't at school today."

"I went to town with my mother."

"Oh. Do you want to come over to my house?"

She huddled back against her knees and didn't answer me.

"You could get sick sitting on the wet ground."

She still didn't answer and her silence made me impatient. "You live in that tan car, don't you?"

"Yes."

"You and your mom?"

"Yes."

Her words came in whispers. Something *was* really wrong with her. "Your dad hasn't sent you any money?" I guessed.

"No. He doesn't have any."

"Well, you want to come to my house for a while? Don't you freeze in that car?"

"I have blankets," she said. "It's all right."

I knelt beside her, trying to see her face again. "Sukey, I have some money. My dad's going to turn in the pawn ticket and he let me keep the thirty-five dollars I saved. You can have it."

"We've got money now."

"You do? Where did you get it?"

"From the pawnshop."

"What did you hock?"

She looked at me then and her eyes were filled with tears. "The guitar."

"Oh, Sukey!" I sank to the ground. "Why did you hock your guitar?"

"Because it was all that was left."

Her words stunned me. I'd thought we were poor, but never this poor. "Maybe when your dad does send money, you can get it back."

"We never get anything back."

This silenced me and I sat beside her with the cold seeping through my jeans. I wished I could think of something else that would make her feel better. I fumbled and fumbled through my mind, but nothing came to me.

Bitsey whined. I took her over to a cedar tree and waited while she squatted under the branches. After she finished, I tugged her back to Sukey. "Please come to my house. I'll make cocoa and cookies. I make awful cookies, but the cocoa's good."

She shook her head, causing her long hair to switch across her hunched shoulders.

"But what will you do without your guitar?"

"I won't sing again."

"Oh, Sukey!"

She pulled herself up and brushed the leaves off her pants. "I have to go."

"Wait a minute. My grandma teaches family life and she knows all about welfare."

Sukey moved away from me. "No, my mother doesn't want to go in a shelter and if they find out about us, the state might take custody of me."

What could I say to that? I watched her walk stiffly toward the road. What else could I do then but brush the leaves from my jeans and drag Bitsey home?

Wishes

While Mom made dinner, I followed her around the kitchen telling her Sukey's story. I was into the Dumpster part when we sat down to eat. Even though I'd been careful not to mention my digging for moldy cinnamon rolls, Grandma listened with a frown.

"What's the matter with that girl's mother? She can get AFDC and food stamps."

"What's AFDC?" I asked.

"Aid to Families with Dependent Children. No child should be eating out of a Dumpster."

"Her mother doesn't want welfare aid because

she's afraid they'll put her in a shelter or take Sukey away from her," I explained.

"Even if a welfare worker did suggest a shelter for them," Grandma said, "she and her mother would only have to stay there until the worker could place them in suitable housing."

"I don't think there's enough housing for all the homeless people," Mom said.

Grandma concentrated on pouring cream into her coffee. "Well, that's true. But if you're persistent, you can find help for a child."

"Maybe you could talk to Sukey's mom," I said.

"I'd be glad to," Grandma said. "You bring her over to meet me."

I nodded even though I didn't have any idea how I'd get Sukey's mom to my house.

Bed is where I get my best ideas. That night I stayed awake until I came up with the plan to invite Sukey and Mrs. Parsons for dinner. I'd say, "My grandma would like to meet your mom. Why don't you come to dinner Friday night?"

No. I'd say, "My mom's making a mess of spaghetti Friday night. I get to invite someone over when she does. Why don't you bring your mom and come to dinner?"

No. I should say, "My mom and grandma would like me to invite you and your mom for dinner. What night can you come?"

That should do it. I went to sleep.

Sukey didn't let me talk to her alone the next day, though. She didn't sit with me on the bus. At recess she played in a soccer game with some of the other sixth graders. I tried to catch up with her when the bell rang, but she ran inside.

She was avoiding me, I knew, because I'd found out more about her life. I would never tell the other kids. And I'd be careful not to act like I was sorry for her again. But she didn't give me a chance.

I put two big potatoes in the oven for Mom and me after I got home from school. Grandma was staying in Seattle for a faculty meeting.

Mom made a salad when she came home. I grated cheese for the potatoes. I didn't bring up Sukey until Mom was settled in her chair.

"My room downstairs is big enough for two kids. Maybe Sukey could—"

Mom held up her hand. "Don't even start. I'm just getting my head above water. And I'm not taking on anything else."

"But what will Sukey do when the guitar money runs out? Somebody has to do something."

"Paula, you can't save all the homeless people and neither can I." She added a stern stare to make me shut up.

The most I dared to do was jab my fork at the chunk of tomato in my salad. Tomato seeds shot across the table. I sneaked a look at Mom. She was busy smearing the melted cheese over her potato.

At night the nightmares came back. I awoke to the sound of knocks on a basement window. It must be Sukey, I thought. She was hungry or cold or something had happened to her mother.

I waved my hand in the dark, trying to find the red ribbon. I had to sit up and whack with both hands before I caught it. There was no one at the windows, though. I shined the flashlight beam through both of them.

Back in my bed, I lay there imagining what it would be like to sleep in a car. How did they do it? You couldn't curl up on the bucket seats in front. Did both Sukey and her mother squeeze together on the back seat?

My feet were cold from walking across the cement floor. It was November and frosty out. Starting up a car to get warm would use gas. I turned over in bed, thinking about my birthday, which is on November 19th. I wished I could have Sukey live with me for my birthday present.

At the breakfast table, I announced. "I thought I heard someone knocking on my window last night."

That got Mom and Grandma's attention.

"I was afraid it was Sukey," I went on. "It's freezing out. How is she going to live in a car all winter?"

Mom sighed. Grandma said, "I thought you were going to bring that girl's mother to see me."

"I was, but she's avoiding me. I think she's embarrassed to have me know she lives in a car."

"Well, try again today," Grandma said. "But if she won't talk to you, we'll call Child Protective."

That sounded scary to me. "The police?"

"No, they're part of social services," Grandma explained. "They take care of children who are in abusive situations."

"I don't think Sukey's abused."

Grandma and Mom exchanged glances.

This wasn't going the way I wanted. "I wish Sukey could live with me."

Mom sighed again. Grandma said, "There's a Chinese saying, 'Be careful what you wish for because it might come true.' "

I excused myself from the table and went downstairs to get my jacket and homework. Sukey was going to talk to me, I decided, even if I had to twist her arm.

When Mr. Loyal took roll, a fourth of the class was absent. "Hmmm, flu season," he said. "We're going to need some substitute lunch workers. Any volunteers?"

"Sukey and I'll do it!" I shouted.

Mr. Loyal lifted his eyebrows.

I hunched down in my seat, gave him a meek smile, and raised my hand to my cheek. "Sir. Please."

That got a smile back. "Okay, you two are it."

I didn't look Sukey's way.

She was quiet while we ate lunch. I pretended not to notice and talked to Kenny the whole time. "How come you have lunch duty so often?" I asked him.

"Free food," he said.

"Lousy food," I said, dropping half of my dry soybean burger back on my tray.

"But free," he repeated, digging into the canned applesauce.

I'd rather have been eating my sack lunch. It had a piece of Grandma's banana cake in it.

Sukey couldn't avoid me while we took the empty trays to the gym. I said, "My mom and grandma want me to invite you and your mom to dinner. What night can you come?"

She stopped pushing her cart and looked at me, her slanted eyes opened wide. "We can't do that. We couldn't invite you back." And before she pushed her cart again, she nodded politely. "Thank you for asking us."

I was disgusted. I'd eaten that crummy school food and missed recess and Mr. Loyal wouldn't choose me for duty again when I had money for lunch and could save the dollar. All the way back to the room I didn't talk to Sukey and she didn't talk to me. I decided I'd rather play with Casey and Kenny. They weren't too proud to take handouts. And with Casey, if you offered him cookies, he'd take three. Even the ones with burned raisins.

I was mad most of the afternoon and lost my place in the reading book when Mr. Loyal called on me. When he called on Sukey, she read in a soft voice while holding her stringy hair back from her face with one hand. From my place across the room, her wrist looked thin enough to snap in two. I stopped being mad and felt sorry for her all over again.

Grandma was late for dinner. She hurried to the table without her usual trip to the bathroom. Mom checked out her watery eyes and mussed hair. "What happened, Mother? Did you have trouble on the freeway?"

"I had a miserable time on the freeway and a miserable time at work. I wish I had a job without smart-mouthed students."

"Be careful what you wish for," I said, "because it might come true."

Ignoring me, Grandma picked out the fattest roll in the bread basket. Her hand shook when she buttered it, I noticed. Mom peered at her with concern. "What happened at school?"

"No matter what you try to do for young people these days, they don't appreciate it."

I had thanked her for making my quilt and curtains, hadn't I? I knew I'd kissed her.

Grandma took a bite of her roll. Her hand was still shaking. Her mussed hair wasn't wet, though, so the kids couldn't have water-bombed her again.

"Mother, you're upset," Mom insisted. "What happened to you?"

"Oh, nothing too unusual. I'd gone to the trouble of ordering cheese and Canadian bacon so my sixth period could make pizzas." Grandma took another bite of roll. I passed her the tuna fish and noodles. She scooped some onto her plate.

"I had all the students busy rolling out their dough," she said, putting down the casserole dish. "The principal was coming in for my evaluation and my room looked nice and the students were on their stools. Then Wolf called out from the back of the room—"

"Wolf?" I said.

"That's the boy's name, Wolf."

Neat name, I said to myself.

"He asked me what shape he should make the pizza. It was a stupid question and I told him to make the shape any way he wanted. I meant round or square, which of course he knew."

"What shape did he make it?" I asked.

"He made an obscene figure."

Obscene? Obscene? While my mind flew over the possibilities, Grandma went on. "I was helping two girls who'd gotten too much flour in their dough, when I heard giggling. I went to the back of the room and saw what he'd done. I told him to throw his dough in the garbage because he'd already gotten an F for the day."

"And he said you'd told him he could make any shape he wanted," I guessed. "Then what did you do?"

"I sent him to the counselor to get transferred to another class. He didn't belong in my room." That seemed to be the end of the story because Grandma began eating her tuna fish and noodles.

"It doesn't sound too bad, Mother," Mom said. "The boy was out of line."

"Of course he was, but John James insisted that wasn't the point."

"Was the principal in your room when you kicked Wolf out?" I knew John James was the principal. Grandma'd had trouble with him before.

"Yes, but I don't know when he came in."

Mom sat looking thoughtful before she asked slowly, "How did your evaluation turn out?"

Grandma put her hand over her mouth. At first I thought it was because she wanted to finish chewing before she answered Mom. Then, when I saw her mouth quiver behind her hand, I knew it was because she was upset. "John told me the enrollment in my classes was getting so low, he didn't know if he could justify keeping me on the staff."

"Oh, dear," Mom said.

I took a gulp of milk to stop myself from asking if Grandma was going to get fired.

Operation Rescue

Grandma and Mom were having coffee and I was clearing the table when Mom said, "Let's all go over and see the new baby."

"We've already done that," I said.

She gave me a look. "Grandma hasn't seen her."

I got it. Grandma needed cheering up. I didn't know how Mom expected that ugly baby to do it, but I went along.

The baby was sleeping. Grandma peeked in the bassinet, but she didn't *ohhh* and *ahhh* like Mom had.

She smiled at Mrs. Willmore and sat back on the couch with Mom and me.

Mrs. Willmore was in her chair with a blanket over her knees. "Are you getting worn out from the night feedings?" Grandma asked her.

"I look awful, don't I?" Mrs. Willmore rubbed her fingers over her saggy face. "The doctor said my uterus dropped. I'm doing some exercises to get it in position."

"I remember those. Mine dropped after having Tessa." Grandma nodded at Mom as if it had been her fault. "I had to keep my nose on the floor and my bottom in the air five times a day."

"Except for exercises, Marleen's supposed to be resting," Mr. Willmore said. "I'm on the road again for three weeks starting next Monday. The doctor suggested a practical nurse, but they're expensive."

"You don't need a nurse," Grandma told him. "You just need a woman to help with the housework and the diapers. And maybe give the baby a bottle in the night until Marleen gets her strength back. Do you have any relatives here?"

"No, they're all in Philadelphia," Mr. Willmore said. "We don't even know many people in Washington."

Grandma turned to Mom. "What about Paula's little homeless friend? Did you meet her mother?"

"I met her briefly at the school talent show," Mom said. "She looked presentable and clean to me."

Oh, oh, I thought, maybe not anymore. Sukey was getting really dirty.

"I don't know about a homeless woman." Mr. Willmore had drawn back in his chair.

"Anybody can be laid off work and lose their home these days," Grandma said. "But it's up to you. If you'd like, I could visit her. And if she seems capable, I could ask her to come see you."

"That might be all right," Mr. Willmore said slowly. "I'm not sure about her having a daughter, though. The woman would have to sleep in the baby's room and we only have a single bed in there."

Better than a car seat, I thought.

On the way back to our house, Mom told Grandma, "I'm not getting involved with a homeless woman and her child. Once you start, you can end up feeling responsible for them."

"That's not the point, Tessa," Grandma said. "This gives me an opportunity to get them to a financial worker. I'll take the woman to DSHS, the Department of Social and Health Services, after she sees the Willmores. I know my way around there. I've been getting students help for thirty years."

It's hard to argue with Grandma, so Mom dropped the subject.

Mom came downstairs that night to kiss me. "This is turning out to be a pretty room," she said, looking at my curtains and cushions.

"It will be better when I get the walls painted. Do you think Grandma can get money for Sukey and her mom?"

"If anybody can, she can."

"It seems funny," I said, "that Grandma has so much trouble with the kids if she helps them so much."

Mom sat on the edge of my bed and smoothed the sheet across my shoulders. "I know. When I was young, I was proud she was my mother. But things changed and she didn't. Her sharp tongue gets the attention. No one notices the nice things she does. You're a little like her, you know."

"No, I'm not!"

Mom laughed. "You don't think you're blunt-spoken and kind?"

"Well, I don't have any trouble getting along with kids and she hasn't any friends."

"She has a friend."

"One. Mrs Logan. Grandma should have taught first grade like Mrs. Logan." I squinted up at Mom. "Will Grandma get fired?"

"They haven't any grounds to fire her. They might find her another job in the school district."

"Doesn't that embarrass her?"

"I think so," Mom said and kissed me good night.

After I climbed on the bus in the morning, I sat down with one of the other kids. I didn't even look up when Sukey got on. Now that Grandma was interested in her, I could back off. I'll say this for Grandma, any project she starts, she finishes.

And just as I expected, as soon as Grandma came home from work that evening, she put the leash on Bitsey and marched back out of the house. I would have loved to follow her. I would have loved to be peeking around a tree when Grandma rapped on the tan car's door. Instead, I did the breakfast dishes, set the table for dinner, and waited.

In less than an hour, I heard Grandma talking to Bitsey on their way up our steps. I leaped to the front door. "What happened? Was Mrs. Parsons in the car?"

Grandma backed into the house, flapping her umbrella open and shut to get rid of the raindrops. She didn't answer me until she'd wiped off Bitsey's feet with a Kleenex from her purse. "Please get me a cup of hot tea," she ordered. "We'll talk at the kitchen table."

I had two cups of water in the microwave and the tea bags out by the time Grandma came in the kitchen. "Well?" I said, settling in a chair across from her and sliding one cup her way.

"Those poor things." She shook her gray head over her steaming tea. "Everything they own was packed into that car. The girl Sukey was in the back seat with her feet propped up on a pile of clothes, trying to do her homework without any light."

"Did Mrs. Parsons invite you in the car?"

"No, but I asked her if we couldn't talk inside out of the rain. Before she could say no, I tied Bitsey's leash to the antenna and opened the door."

"I wish I could have seen you barging in. Sukey's good at holding me off."

Grandma took a sip of tea and shook her head some more. "You can't blame her. It's pitiful. The only food I saw was a half carton of chocolate milk and a package of hot dog buns."

"She probably got the buns out of the Dumpster. But what about welfare and Mrs. Willmore's job?"

"Mrs. Parsons is going to see Mrs. Willmore tomorrow and I'm going to make an appointment for us with DSHS."

"Wow, Grandma, you're fast."

Grandma allowed a pleased look to pass over her face before she took another sip of tea and said, "Well, that woman's in a desperate situation."

"I guess. Was she clean enough to see Mrs. Willmore?"

"She was rumpled, but I'm sure she has sense enough to wash up at a gas station first." Grandma pushed her cup away from her. "This is Wednesday.

Your mother works an hour later tonight. We'd better start dinner."

"Wait a minute. Wait one more minute." I was waving both hands at Grandma. "What about Sukey? What if she can't stay at the Willmores'?"

"You want her to stay here? You'd better think that over carefully, miss. You're an only child and you're not used to sharing."

"Sukey's an only child, too. And I can share. But Mom doesn't want her."

"It isn't Sukey your mother doesn't want, it's more expenses. But a good social worker can come up with clothes and medical coupons and food stamps for the Parsonses."

"Then there's no problem," I said.

Grandma got up to start dinner. I put our tea cups in the sink, thinking how much fun it was going to be with Sukey for a sister.

Nailing the Chevy

I expected Grandma to tell Mom about her visit with Mrs. Parsons. She didn't. I waited all through dinner, but the two of them got off on Californians migrating to Washington and what that did to real estate prices and the job market. I wiggled in my chair and picked at my food, but they went on and on about the population explosion on the I-5 corridor.

I should have paid attention so I'd have something to say during current events. I should have at least waited until Grandma chose the right time to bring up the subject of Mrs. Parsons to Mom. I didn't.

When Mom and Grandma paused to pour themselves more coffee, I said, "Mom, Grandma saw Mrs. Parsons today."

Mom said, "Oh, how did that come out?"

"I think Mrs. Willmore will be pleased with her." Grandma kept her voice in neutral.

"And is Mr. Willmore pleased to have her daughter live with them?" Mom's voice was sharp and I should have shut up right then.

Instead, I said, "There's plenty of room downstairs for Sukey to stay with me if he doesn't want her."

Mom pinned me with glittering eyes. "Paula, you don't know what you're talking about. It would be insane of me to take another child. Now that the bills are finally paid, I need to start a savings account. What do you think would happen if I lost my job?"

"There's Dad."

"Yes, there's your dad, but he works in the Northwest's dying industry."

"The mill's going full-time."

"Now it is."

I looked at Grandma, hoping she'd tell Mom about the food stamps and medical coupons, but Grandma gave me a shake of her head. I finally got the message and shut up.

Sukey wasn't at her bus stop the next morning. As the bus pulled away without her, a boy yelled from a back seat. "Hey, the cops are nailing that Chevy."

I stared out the window to see Sukey, her mom, and a policeman standing beside the tan car. A patrol car was parked behind them with the radio blaring police calls.

My stomach sank. And it stayed sick the whole day. On the bus going home, I checked the street for the tan car. It wasn't there.

I took Bitsey for her walk and then tried to watch TV until Mom or Grandma came home. I was changing channels for the tenth time when Mom arrived. "You don't have to worry about taking in another kid," I told her. "The police have Sukey."

Mom took off her coat and hung it on the stand by the door. "How do you know?"

"Because I saw them with the police this morning. And their car's gone now."

"Oh. Well, the police may be the best ones to take care of the problem."

"How do you know?"

Before she could snap back at me, Grandma came in the door.

"You're too late," I told her. "The police have Sukey."

Grandma took off her coat and patted Bitsey. "Let's have a cup of tea."

"I don't want any tea," I said and headed for the basement.

"Yes, you will," Grandma called after me. "And we'll need a kettle full."

I felt like ignoring her and stamping on downstairs, but my brains jerked the reins on my feelings. I grabbed the tea kettle, filled it with water, and slapped it on the stove. And then waited for Grandma and Mom to join me at the kitchen table.

When she sat down, Mom didn't seem to be in any better mood than I was. Grandma had that "I know something you don't know" look on her face. She took two sips of her tea before she started talking.

"I met Mrs. Parsons at DSHS after work—"

"But what about the police?" I asked.

"They told Mrs. Parsons she couldn't stay parked on the Machias Road. She explained that she has a live-in job starting Monday so they didn't do more than warn her to move her car. She's parking it behind the post office until Monday morning when she takes it over to the Willmores'."

"That job is only for three weeks," Mom put in.

"It's a start," Grandma said. "Three weeks will give her time to look for more work and the financial worker time to try to find permanent shelter for her and her daughter."

"Can she?" I asked.

"We'll see. One thing at a time. Mrs. Willmore is going to pay Mrs. Parsons ten dollars a day plus room and board. And Mrs. Parsons is going to give you half of that, Tessa. I don't think the girl will cost you more than five dollars a day."

Mom drew circles on the table with her spoon. "I'm not trying to be a mean woman. But I'm afraid that once I take the girl in, I'll be left responsible for her. How can I put her back on the street after she's lived with us?"

"I've made it clear to Mrs. Parsons that you will provide care for three weeks only. And we can agree here with that, too. Can't we?" Grandma raised her eyebrows at me.

I shrugged. "I guess I have to say yes."

Mom kept drawing her circles. "That isn't good enough. I don't enjoy your thinking of me as Scrooge, Paula."

"I don't think of you as Scrooge, but Sukey's getting skinnier and skinnier."

Silence.

"I agree to three weeks," I said. "I promise I won't make a fuss."

Early Monday morning, Mrs. Parsons pulled into the Willmores' driveway. Before I helped Sukey haul in her stuff, I took a good look at Mrs. Parsons.

Her blond hair was pulled into a rubber band, not fluffed around her head as it had been the night of the talent show. Maybe apples and doughnuts weren't enough for her either, because her dress sagged over her chest. But her dress was clean and so was her face. She thanked me for sharing my room with Sukey.

"I'm glad to," I said, leaning into the back seat to gather up Sukey's books. Sukey wasn't saying anything as she scuttled between the car and my room. She only gave a shy nod to Grandma and Mom when they tried to welcome her.

While I put her books in my bookcase and she shoved her underclothes in my bottom dresser drawer, I tried to be friendly. "It's going to be great having you live here. We can paint the walls cream together, huh?"

Sukey's eyes swiveled sideways to glance at the walls, but she said nothing. I planned to get the whole story of her life out of her in bed that night. We'd talk together before we fell asleep, I was sure.

At school, Melody, a girl in our room, got off her bus at the same time Sukey and I climbed down from ours. "Hey, Melody," I yelled, "meet my new roommate."

Sukey stiffened beside me. I think she was afraid I might tell Melody I'd taken in a homeless girl. I told Melody Sukey's mom was caring for a baby next door so Sukey got to stay with me.

"You two will have a blast," Melody said. "Sukey, are you going to teach Paula how to play your guitar?"

Before Sukey could answer, Karen poked herself

into the middle of our group and wanted to know what was going on. "Sukey gets to live with me while her mom works next door," I explained.

Karen didn't say much about that until we got in our classroom. She waited until I sat down before she leaned my way and wrinkled her nose as if she smelled something bad. "You're letting *her* stay at *your* house?"

Karen was the only one in the room who put down Sukey. It didn't really matter what Karen thought. No one paid attention to her opinions.

That night, I asked Sukey if she wanted to take a shower before or after I did. "I'm too tired," she said, leaning her hand on my soft bed. "I think I'll go to sleep."

She looked tired. But the dark circles under her eyes always made her look that way. When I came back downstairs in my bathrobe, Sukey was sound asleep.

She was flopped on her back in the middle of my bed. I squeezed in beside her, squirmed around her arms and legs, and then decided that this would not do. I pulled up my knees, planted my feet on her hip, and gently pushed until she half woke up and rolled over.

At first, I lay on my left side facing her. But I could smell her that way so I turned over to my right side.

She'd have to take a shower before we went to bed the next night. I hoped she hadn't stunk up the sheets.

When my radio alarm rang in the morning, Sukey crawled out of bed and pulled her jeans on over the underpants she'd slept in. I watched her from my pillow, trying not to scrunch up my face the way Karen had. "Aren't you going to change your clothes?"

Sukey's pale face turned red. She pushed her jeans back down to her feet in a hurry. "I guess I thought I was still in our cold car," she said.

I got dressed, gathered my dirty clothes, and picked up Sukey's with two fingers. I deposited them all in the washer and turned it on before breakfast. Grandma had pancakes for us. Sukey took one every time Grandma passed her the platter. I stuffed the clothes in the dryer before we went to school and took them out when we got home. Sukey helped me put them away.

Grandma baked a cherry pie for dinner. Sukey said it was delicious three times and scraped every drop of cherry juice off her plate. Grandma beamed at her. I was getting the idea that what Grandma liked was doing things for kids who were grateful.

When we were getting up from the table, I told Sukey she didn't have to help with the dishes because she'd probably want to wash her hair. She blushed again, covered her sticky hair with her hands, and rushed into the bathroom. Mom didn't say anything, but Grandma shot me a frown before she carried the leftover pie to the refrigerator.

I hadn't asked for seconds for Sukey and me, because I knew Grandma liked taking pie to school for her lunch. While I was doing dishes all by myself, I was thinking that I was a thoughtful kid. I just didn't slobber over people with compliments.

Mom, Grandma, and I were watching a TV movie when Sukey came into the living room with a towel wrapped around her head. Grandma looked up at her. "Why don't I cut your hair while it's wet?"

Sukey took a step back. "Short?"

"Oh, no," Grandma said. "We'll just trim the ends and cut your bangs."

"She's good," I told Sukey. "She does mine."

Grandma and Sukey went into the kitchen for the haircut and Mom and I went on watching the movie.

Half an hour later, Grandma asked, "What do you think?"

Mom and I turned from the TV to look over Sukey. Sukey's bangs had been hanging halfway down the side of her face. Now they were fanned across the tops of her eyebrows. The rest of her shiny dark hair floated to her shoulders.

"You look like a China doll," Mom said.

"You do," I agreed.

"Yes," Grandma said. "Where did you get those eyes?"

"I am part Chinese," Sukey said. "My dad is half Chinese."

"What does he do?" Grandma asked.

"He's a cook. He was cooking in a Chinese restaurant in Yakima until he got sick. We had to bring him to Seattle for an operation. When he came out of the hospital, he couldn't work for six weeks and they hired a new cook in the restaurant and . . ." Sukey's voice faded away.

"Come sit down with us," Mom said, "and watch the film."

"No, thank you. I think I'd like to go to bed." Sukey gave us her little nod and left for the basement.

I would have gone with her, but I wanted to see the end of the movie. When I got downstairs, she was sound asleep, flat on her back again. Luckily, she didn't weigh much and it was easy to push her over to her side.

In the morning, when we combed our hair in my dresser mirror, I saw that the circles were gone from under her eyes. At school, even Mr. Loyal noticed how pretty she looked. "Been to the local beauty parlor?" he asked her, as he passed out the ditto sheets for our history chapter.

Sukey ran her hand over the back of her hair. "No. Paula's grandma cut it."

He looked across the room at me. "Good job."

I looked over at Karen and gave her my nastiest smirk.

As soon as Sukey and I got home from school, her mother called. Mrs. Willmore was at the doctor's and Mrs. Parsons wanted Sukey to come over for a visit. "You come, too," Sukey said to me after she hung up.

"No, I'll do my homework. You probably want to talk to your mom."

"You can talk to her, too." Sukey pulled me by the hand. "Come on. She said she baked cookies."

Mrs. Parsons was changing the baby when we got there. She wrapped it in a clean blanket and held it up for Sukey to see. Sukey took the baby's tiny fingers in hers. "She's cute."

I still wouldn't have called it cute, but at least the red blotches were gone from its face.

Mrs. Parsons put the baby back in its bassinet and made us a pot of cocoa. There were raisin oatmeal cookies in a plate on the kitchen table which I eyed until the cocoa was ready. Mrs. Parsons passed the plate and we each took one cookie.

"You hair looks nice," she said to Sukey.

"Paula's grandma did it."

I thought Mrs. Parsons's hair looked nice, too, fluffed around her head again. "I'm grateful Sukey found a friend like you," she said to me. "Until her daddy gets steady work, we're on our own."

"There aren't any other girls in this neighborhood," I said. "I wanted a friend, too."

Mrs. Parsons bit into her cookie, smiling to herself. "You know, the best part of this job is the bathroom. The first night I stayed under the shower until I was pink."

"I went to sleep," Sukey said. "Paula's got the biggest, softest bed."

Mrs. Parsons turned again to me. Her eyes were so blue they looked like flowers. "Sukey tells me you made a room in your basement."

I nodded. "My dad did. I'll visit him this weekend. But next weekend, Sukey and I can paint the walls so the place will be ready for my birthday."

"You girls are almost the same age. Sukey's birthday is three days before Christmas."

"That's terrible," I said. "Nobody'll want to give you two presents."

"Tell me about it," Sukey said.

Mrs. Parsons pushed at Sukey's hand. "Oh, you always get remembered on your birthday."

When we'd finished our cookies and cocoa, Mrs. Parsons rose from the table. "I'd better get this kitchen cleaned up before Mrs. Willmore comes home."

That sounded like a good idea to me. The kitchen sink was full of dishes, probably the lunch ones and breakfast ones, too. Maybe the baby took up a lot of time. "We'll help," I offered.

Sukey cleared the table, Mrs. Parsons washed, and I dried. The first time Mrs. Parsons handed me a plate that had a smear of egg on it, I wiped it clean with the dishtowel. The second time, I handed it back to her. "There's still egg on this."

"Oh, dear," she said. "I can hardly see anything without my glasses."

"Where are they?" I asked.

"I sat on them," Sukey said.

"You sat on them?"

"She did," Mrs. Parsons said. "But I should have watched where I put them down when I got ready for bed. There wasn't much room in the car, you know."

I knew.

Sukey gave her mom a big hug when we left. Mrs. Parsons kissed her with tears in her eyes. "Be a good girl."

"Your mom's nice," I said on the way home.

"I think so," Sukey said.

"I Might Be Dead"

Dad phoned during dinner Friday evening. He wanted to be sure he was picking me up the next morning. "Of course," I told him.

Back at the table, Mom asked, "Did you tell your father to expect a guest?"

"A guest?" I didn't know what she was talking about.

Mom kept her concentration on me, making me remember my manners.

"Oh, I thought Sukey would rather stay here so she could visit her mother."

A flush crept over Sukey's face. Seeing that, Mom's eyes glittered warningly.

"Well, it doesn't make any difference," I said. "Sukey can come with me if she wants to. Dad's easy."

"Call him back," Mom said.

I smashed down my napkin and marched to the phone.

Sukey's face stayed flushed all through dessert. She didn't tell Grandma her apple cobbler was delicious. She helped me do the dishes, but she didn't say anything when I told her she'd like my dad. After we finished cleaning the kitchen, she went downstairs. I watched TV a little bit, but Mom had on the news, and I kept feeling guilty about Sukey. Grandma wasn't helping with her pursed lips. I went downstairs.

Sukey was sitting on the edge of the bed, staring at her folded hands.

"How come you're down here?" I asked.

"I'll sleep in our car this weekend," she said, still looking at her hands.

"You can't do that. Grandma would kill me."

"We can tell her and your mom that I'm staying at another girl's house."

"No." I sat on the bed with her. "Listen, Sukey, I'm a pig about my dad. I can't even stand it when that one-finger sawyer comes to the movies with us."

"I won't bother you. I'll stay in my car." The final way she said it scared me.

"Sukey." I tried to put my hand on her shoulder, but she shrank away. "Oh, crap! Oh, Sukey. My mom makes me mad sometimes, but I didn't mean to hurt your feelings. It was my idea to have you stay with us. I didn't mean to mess it up. You go to my dad's with me, okay?"

Sukey shook her head and that made me desperate. What else could I say to make things better? I leaned across my bed, turned on my radio, and switched it from one station to another, trying to figure out how to put things back together. The only thing I could think of was to beg.

I turned the radio off and sat up. "Sukey, please, please, please come with me. I know I've been a jerk. I couldn't eat for a week after my mom kicked my dad out. I know you've had it a million times worse than I have. And it was mean of me to want to hog my dad, but I didn't want to hurt your feelings. Listen, I'll do anything. I'll do the dishes every night by myself. I'll do all your homework. I'll sing for you."

Sukey couldn't help it. She smiled. She'd heard me sing at the talent show. I'm awful.

Even though she agreed to go with me, Sukey was a little shy when Dad picked us up. He had her giggling by the time we reached Arlington. He teased her about her lotus-blossom eyes and said she'd have to teach him how to use chopsticks.

We went to a Chinese restaurant for dinner and it turned out she really could use chopsticks. So could Dad. I fumbled around dropping rice on the tablecloth until Sukey adjusted my fingers.

She told me in bed that night that my dad was cool. "He is," I said. "My mom's okay, but I've always liked my dad best."

Sukey was quiet a minute before she said, "I guess I like mine both the same. Why did your folks break up, anyway?"

"Dad was in a tavern with Leslie, the bevel sawyer, and Mom caught them. She completely lost it. Dad didn't have a chance. I think maybe he'd talked himself back some other times and this was it with her." I punched my pillow into a more comfortable shape for my head. "How come you and your mom aren't with your dad?"

"We were supposed to be. After Dad lost his cooking job in Yakima, he couldn't find one around Seattle. His cousin wrote him to come to San Francisco because there were more Chinese restaurants there. Mom'd found a job checking in a grocery store so Dad took a bus to California. We were going to follow him as soon as he was cooking again.

"Then Mom hurt her back carrying out fifty pounds of dog food and we got behind in our apartment payments. We moved to a motel to rent by the week, but Dad still didn't have steady work. When our money was gone, we just parked our car here and lived in it."

"Didn't your mom try for another job?"

"When the chiropractor said she could, she did. But he told her not to lift more than ten pounds or her back would go out again. Mom walked all over looking for work, but she couldn't find any."

"What a mess of bad luck," I said.

"Ya," Sukey agreed. "It seemed like bad things happened and kept happening."

"You haven't been going to the post office every day, though."

"Mom goes now when she shops for Mrs. Willmore." Sukey sighed and turned over. "Beds are nice."

We were sleeping on Dad's pull-out couch and it seemed lumpy to me.

Sukey gave out one more long sigh and fell asleep.

We had lunch at Rotten Ralph's the next day. I decided on a fishwich and a blackberry shake. Dad looked down at Sukey while she studied the wall menu and prices. "What'll it be for you?" he asked.

"I guess I'll have a chicken sandwich."

"And what do you want to drink?"

She answered him in a small voice. "Water's fine."

He dropped his hand on her shoulder. "Listen,

Sukey, we have a problem here. While we were driving in the truck, I worried because I heard my motor knocking."

Dad had on his serious face and Sukey looked up at him with concern.

"Then," Dad said, "I realized my motor wasn't knocking. Your bones were rattling."

For a second, Sukey didn't get it. Then she clapped a hand over her mouth to cover her burst of laughter.

"Come on," Dad said. "You'd better have an ice cream shake."

"I'll try a blackberry one like Paula," she agreed.

Dad drove us home after lunch. On the way, he asked me what I wanted for my birthday.

"A guitar," I said.

"Are you sure?" He turned from his driving to glance at me. "I didn't know you were interested in playing music."

"Just an acoustic guitar. Sukey can teach me." I gave her a poke. "Huh, Sukey?"

"I'll try," Sukey said.

Before we got out of his truck, he gave me his grandmother's bracelet. "Here. See if you can hold on to it this time."

"Don't worry. I will." After I kissed him goodbye, I stuck the bracelet in my pocket so Mom wouldn't see it. And as soon as I went down to the basement, I put it in my jewelry box.

Sukey and I didn't wait until the next Saturday to paint the walls in my room because Mom wanted me to celebrate my birthday then. She said she'd better be home if I was going to have my usual noisy party. "Why don't you invite all girls this year?" she suggested.

"I can't leave Casey out," I objected. "And anyway he has to see the clean walls so he'll want to decorate them."

"Not with more of that spray painting, I hope," Grandma said.

"No, Sukey and I like his drawings best. And we can play Pin the Tail on the Donkey. He can draw the donkey."

"Isn't that game a little young for your crowd?" Grandma said.

"Not if Casey does the donkey," I told her. "Can you bring us a big sheet of butcher paper from your school? And will you make us a boxful of your yummy fudge for a prize?"

"Well. I might manage that," Grandma said.

I thought she would. And she did. Friday night, Sukey and I had the butcher paper taped to one of the cream-colored walls, the box of fudge wrapped with a ribbon, and strings of balloons hanging from the beams. My savings were down to twenty-two dollars, but I didn't care.

"How does it look?" I asked Sukey when I came back in the room from putting the stool away.

Sukey was on the bed staring at the mass of balloons. "Fantastic!" she said.

I flopped down beside her. "You're right," I said. "Fantastic."

I had invited Melody, Evelyn, Casey, Nick, and Kenny. I left out Karen, even though I'd known her since kindergarten. "Are you going to have a party this year?" she'd asked after she saw me giving Evelyn an invitation.

"Yes, but I knew you wouldn't want to come because Sukey will be there."

What could she say? I thought it was pretty funny and wanted to tell Sukey about it. I couldn't, though. It might have hurt her feelings.

Dad sneaked in the back door and down to the basement before Sukey and I were up Saturday morning. I didn't know who was jiggling the bolt until I unlatched it. "Daddy! What have you got?"

He whipped the guitar from behind his back. "Presto! Your present."

"Wow! You did it." I threw my arms around him and hugged him.

The guitar was made of lighter wood than Sukey's had been and it had a fake snakeskin strap. After I strummed it once, I took it to the bed, where Sukey was watching us with a solemn face. "Play something so we can hear how it sounds," I said.

Sukey played a few chords, then turned the pegs and plucked each string. "It's out of tune," she explained.

Dad sat on the bed with us. "I bought it second-hand in a music store and I wouldn't know which one was out of tune."

"They probably all were if customers fiddled with them," Sukey said. "There. That's better."

"Play something. Play something," I said.

Sukey played "She'll Be Comin' Around the Mountain."

"Sing," I insisted.

Sukey sang.

The door of my room opened. Mom stood there. She was in her low-cut nylon nightgown and her auburn hair was tumbled and her cheeks were rosy. "Oh. You're here, Carter."

Dad stood up. "I brought Paula her birthday present. I'll leave now."

"No, that's fine. I just wondered . . ."

I leaped off the bed and hugged Dad again. "Thank you! Thank you. That's a great present."

He hugged me back and then carefully walked around Mom to go out the door.

Grandma and Mom gave me their presents at

breakfast. Grandma gave me a huge, round, cream-colored lantern to hang over my bare light bulb. Mom gave me a red rug to place beside my bed.

"Oh, Sukey, now our room's going to be even more fantastic for the party." I reached over to her chair and poked her in the ribs. "Hurry up and eat so we can take my presents downstairs."

She gave me her shy smile and slipped a folded paper toward my plate of half-eaten French toast. "Here. I wrote a poem for you."

In the middle of a big heart was printed:

> *Paula has the softest bed*
> *The coolest head*
> *And I might be dead*
> *But she rescued me instead.*

Hear the Wind Blow

"Hey, man!" Kenny yelled, letting popcorn dribble out of his mouth. "You've got it all wrong. Mules have long legs. A donkey has short legs."

"Hmmm." Casey stood back from his drawing. "This game is now Pin the Tail on the Mule."

"I'm first," Nick said. "What did you say the prize was, Paula?"

"A box of Grandma's fudge."

"That's what I thought you said. Blindfold me. I'm going to stick the pin right on the end of that mule's butt."

I handed him the paper tail marked "Nick," Melody tied the scarf over his eyes, and Evelyn twirled him around. He walked straight into my bed, banging his knee against the end board. He swore and we all laughed.

Melody was next. She drove her pin into the mule's stomach. Evelyn hit the wall, Kenny pinned the mule's front leg, I pinned his back leg, and Sukey pinned the sky.

"Way off. You guys are way off. Watch me cool this." Casey took the scarf from Sukey.

"Oh, no you don't." Melody sprang off my bed, snatched the scarf from him, and tied it over his face.

I was the one who twirled him around and I made it a triple twirl. Casey inched toward the wall. Slowly, slowly, with his arms outstretched, he closed in on the mule. "You can't touch the paper," I said. "That's cheating."

"I'm not going to touch the paper," he mumbled through the scarf. "And you aren't going to win, Paula."

"I am if you cheat."

I watched him. All of us watched him. He nudged one foot forward until it bumped against the wall. "Hey!" I yelled.

"It's okay," Nick said from his perch on Grandma's piano bench. "He's just keeping himself from crashing."

Casey carefully waved his left hand over the paper until it brushed my pin, making it and my tail fall to the floor.

I made a move toward Casey. Nick jumped off the bench and grabbed me. "He didn't touch the paper! He didn't touch the paper!"

Casey shoved his pin in the mule and ripped the scarf from his face. When he saw his tail hanging from the mule's hind end, he danced in a circle with his hands clasped above his head. "The winner is *me!*"

Nick took the box of fudge off my brass trunk and, bowing low to Casey, held out the prize. Casey tore away the wrapping, checked the inside of the box, and replaced the cover.

"You gotta pass it around, man," Nick told him.

"No way," Casey said. "I won it. I eat it."

"You're sleazy, Casey," I said.

"No I'm not. I'm smart."

Mom came in the door, carrying two six-packs of root beer, napkins, and a tablecloth. Grandma was behind her with a steaming pizza in each hand. Kenny's eyes lit up at the sight of the food.

"Here, let me help you, Mrs. Tomlin." Kenny took the tablecloth from Mom's arm and spread it on the floor. It was his only try at being polite. He grabbed the first slice of pizza and ate the last one. He even helped me blow out the candles on the cake so I'd hurry up and cut it.

When the last lick of ice cream on his plate was gone, he rolled over and climbed on the piano bench.

"And the pig got up and slowly walked away," sang Melody.

"Now what'll we do?" Nick asked.

Evelyn pointed to my guitar, which was hanging on the shingles above Kenny. "Can you play your new guitar, Paula?"

"Two chords. G and D. Sukey taught me those this morning."

"Sukey, play," Melody ordered.

"Ya. Play the pickle song." Kenny reached up to take down the guitar.

Melody carried it to Sukey, who was sitting in my rocker. Sukey always sat in my rocker. It was the only comfortable chair in the room.

She played the pickle song and "She'll Be Comin' Around the Mountain." Nick clicked his tongue and cracked an imaginary whip as Sukey sang, "She'll be driving six white horses when she comes, when she comes. She'll be be driving six white horses when she comes."

"More!" the kids pleaded until Sukey played a song with the words "Hang your head over and hear the wind blow." After the third verse all the kids joined in. I didn't.

I was lying on my bed with my chin on my hand,

watching everyone crowded on the floor below Sukey.
Casey glanced my way a couple of times. When Sukey
paused again, strumming the guitar softly, Casey said,
"How about 'Happy Birthday'?"

"Yes," Melody agreed, "let's sing to Paula."

The kids turned around and sang "Happy Birthday" at me, which just made me feel dumb.

I got back into the birthday spirit after Sukey put
the guitar down and Evelyn clicked the tape of Paula
Abdul into my clock radio. It was her present to me
and she'd written on the card, "Paula for Paula." As
the music hit the room, Casey held his hand out to
me. "Come on, let's dance."

I was the only one Casey danced with. All the girls
like him best. Nick's funny, but the top of his head
comes to our eyebrows and everything Kenny pigs
down fattens his pumpkin bottom.

After the kids left, Sukey and I dumped the paper
plates, napkins, and root beer cans into the middle of
the tablecloth and hauled it upstairs. Grandma and
Mom were drinking coffee in the kitchen. "How did
the party go?" Grandma asked us. "Did everyone like
my fudge?"

"Nobody got to taste it," I told her. "Casey won
and he wouldn't pass it around."

"Casey only danced with Paula," Sukey said.

Grandma nodded at me. "Naturally you'd like him
best. He looks like your dad."

"Casey has black hair," I said, "but he also has freckles and Dad doesn't."

"He'll grow out of the freckles," Grandma said, "but they never grow out of those wild eyes."

Mom kept her attention on her coffee cup while we were talking. She did look up to say, "Don't put the root beer cans in the garbage, Paula. Put them in the recycling bin."

On my way out the back door to the bin, I met Mrs. Willmore. "Is your mother home?" she asked me.

"She's in the kitchen. Go on in."

I didn't want to get trapped listening to stories about Mrs. Willmore's uterus or her ugly baby. As soon as I had the cans stashed, Sukey and I went to my room.

I flopped on the bed because Sukey took my rocker, again. "Did my mom seem kinda down to you?"

Sukey wrinkled her nose while she thought that over. "Well, she looked disappointed this morning when your dad left."

"I know. And her cheeks aren't naturally red. She says she has olive French skin. I bet she put blush on because she knew Dad was here."

"Maybe they'll get back together."

"No, she's been too mean to him too long. She should have started being nice about a year ago. He's settled into his bachelor life now."

"Do you care?"

"Not anymore. Every two weeks, I get *all* of his attention. If he lived here, Mom would want him to do things with her."

Sukey bobbed her head in agreement and gave the rocker a big swing. I picked up the miniature chess game Nick had given me. "Let's play."

We sat on the floor together and tried two games, but Sukey couldn't remember which way the knights and bishops moved. I folded the board and took down my guitar. Sukey showed me where to put my fingers for the A and C chords, but when she tried to get me to play a tune, I kept messing up.

"Let's take our showers," I said. "I'm hopeless."

The walls in our old house are thin. You can hear everything that happens in the next room. Just as I put my hand on the kitchen door, Mrs. Willmore's voice came through the wall. ". . . but I don't see how I can keep her. She serves the food on dirty dishes."

I turned quickly around to see if Sukey had heard. She had. She backed down the stairs.

Sukey sat in the rocker with her towel on her lap. She kept trembling and saying, "Bad things are happening again. Bad things are starting to happen again."

"Listen, Sukey." I was kneeling in front of her, trying to get her attention. "Your mom just needs some glasses. That doesn't mean . . ."

I didn't know how to finish. I couldn't say it didn't mean she'd be back sleeping in her car or she'd be eating out of a Dumpster again. Those were the words that flashed in my mind, but they were too scary to say.

"I'm going upstairs to talk to Grandma," I said.

I marched past Mom and Mrs. Willmore, who were sitting at the kitchen table, and into the living room, where Grandma was reading. "Mrs. Willmore's going to fire Sukey's mom."

Grandma put down her book. "What makes you think so?"

"Because that's what she's telling Mom in the kitchen."

"There must be a reason," Grandma said.

So I told her the whole story, starting with my wiping the dishes for Mrs. Parsons and ending with Sukey downstairs trembling in the rocker.

Grandma shook her gray head. "No, no, no. They are not going to be back on the street. Mrs. Parsons is eligible for the Medically Needy Program. She should discuss the broken glasses with her financial worker, who will explain the procedure for getting new ones."

"But how long will that take?"

"I imagine it will be several days before her prescription is filled."

I threw out my hands in front of Grandma. "But that might be too late."

Grandma shook her head again. "Mrs. Willmore

only needs help for one more week. Mrs. Parsons needs to be planning for another position anyway."

"I hope she is," I said. "And I hope she gets one before she's fired."

Grandma rose from the couch. "I'll talk to Mrs. Parsons tomorrow and I'll go talk to Mrs. Willmore now."

I followed Grandma into the kitchen, trying to keep a pleased smirk off my face as I passed the table.

Downstairs, Sukey was still slumped in the rocker.

"Grandma's going to fix it," I told her. "She's going to tell your mom how to get free glasses and she's explaining everything to Mrs. Willmore right now."

"Really? Your grandma has to be the Clint Eastwood of all grandmas." Sukey wiped the back of her hand across the tears on her face. "Can I play your guitar for a little while?"

She played it for more than a little while because I fell asleep to her music.

The Guitar

"Doesn't Mrs. Willmore go to church on Sunday morning?" Grandma asked. She was sitting on the couch, reading the business section of the paper.

Mom was beside her, reading the entertainment section. "Every single Sunday," she answered.

"I think I'll trot over to see the baby." Grandma folded the paper and went into her bedroom. When Bitsey saw her come out wearing a coat, she danced around the living room.

"No, no, you have to stay home," Grandma said. "Puppy dogs might scare little babies."

Bitsey whined.

Grandma patted her head. "If you're a good girl, I'll take you for a walk this afternoon."

Bitsey crawled under the coffee table to sulk as Grandma went out the door.

"Trade ya," I said to Sukey, holding out my half of the funnies. Sukey traded.

We lay on the floor reading. Or at least I was reading. When I opened the paper to the inside pages, Sukey was still on *Calvin and Hobbes*. When I turned the paper over to read the back, Sukey still stared at the tiger.

She was waiting for Grandma to return. That's what she was doing. She was waiting and worrying about her mom.

Grandma came in the door and I said, "That didn't take you long."

Sukey looked from me to Grandma.

"Your mother is going to get her glasses," Grandma told her.

"Will . . . will . . . will Mrs. Willmore wait?" Sukey stuttered.

"Oh, yes. After church she's taking your mother up to the drugstore to buy reading glasses. They'll do for a few days." Grandma kneeled down to peer at Bitsey under the table. "Come on, you silly thing. We'll go for a walk now."

"Thanks very much," Sukey called after Grandma

and Bitsey. Then she asked me, "Can I play your guitar some more?"

"Sure," I said, "since I'm too dumb to learn how."

"You aren't too dumb," she objected. "It just takes a lot of practice."

Sukey went downstairs and I gathered up the funnies. With a raised eyebrow, Mom handed me the entertainment section. "Breakfast dishes?"

"Ugh. You should have reminded me before I let Sukey play my guitar. She won't put it down for hours."

I was right. After I finished the dishes, I found Sukey still playing and humming along with herself. "What's the name of that tune?" I asked her.

"It doesn't have name a yet." She squinted at the ceiling. "Maybe I'll call it 'The Traveling Song.' "

Traveling was what she was hoping to do, I thought. And that must have been what Mrs. Parsons was hoping, too. Sukey stopped to visit her when we took Bitsey for a walk the next day.

I let Bitsey lead me into the woods and down to the creek. There was ice on the edge of the frosty bank. I stood watching the water tumble over the gray stones while Bitsey sniffed bare bushes and finally squatted on a pile of fallen leaves.

Sukey met us at the edge of the woods. "I'm glad I don't have to go to the bathroom in there anymore."

"Your bottom would freeze," I said. "How's your mom? Has she lined up another place?"

"Not yet, but she had a letter from Daddy. He has a temporary job in a new restaurant. If they like his cooking, they might keep him on permanently."

"I bet she hopes they do."

"So do I," Sukey said.

As we walked back to my house, I thought my mom would be going crazy if her job was ending in five days and Dad's was on trial. I'd be so worried I wouldn't be able to sit still. Sukey did.

She sat in my rocker and plucked away at her traveling song before dinner and after dinner and before we went to bed. I guess it was the right song because we'd barely gotten home from school the next afternoon when Mrs. Parsons knocked on the back door. I opened it and when Sukey saw who I let in, she said, "Is something the matter, Mom?"

Mrs. Parsons held out a letter. "See for yourself."

It wasn't bad news. I could tell that from the way Mrs. Parsons's smiling mouth hung open while she watched Sukey read the letter.

"Daddy's got the job!" Sukey threw her arms around her mom. "We're off to California! How much money did he send?"

"One hundred and twenty dollars."

"One hundred and twenty dollars! We'll go first-class."

"Well, I still have to pay Paula's mother for your food."

"But didn't Mrs. Willmore pay you?" Sukey asked.

"Yes, we'll have that, too." Mrs. Parsons paused a minute, her blue eyes sparkling as if she were saving the best news for last. "How soon can you get ready?"

"Today? We're going today? I'll be ready in ten minutes." Sukey shoved the letter at her mom and flew out the kitchen door and down the basement steps.

Mrs. Parsons opened her purse. "Your mother was charging me five dollars a day for Sukey. It's been fourteen days. Give this seventy dollars to her for me, please."

I took the money reluctantly, wishing my mom hadn't charged her anything. "Does Mrs. Willmore mind you leaving before her husband gets back?"

"I don't think so. She feels better now and she needs to get used to taking care of the baby herself."

"That'd be hard. It's such an ugly thing."

Mrs. Parsons laughed. "Yes, isn't she."

I had the thought that even though she was poor, Mrs. Parsons would be fun on a trip. "Are you all packed?"

"All packed and with the car waiting in front of your house," she said.

They were leaving. Really, really leaving. I went slowly down the basement steps.

Sukey was throwing her clothes into a black plastic garbage bag. "Do you mind if I use this thing?" she asked.

"No. No. Mom has a whole box of those bags." As I watched her stick in the last of her underwear, I wanted to ask if she'd miss me. It seemed too dumb to say.

Sukey threw the bag over her shoulder. "Wowee! Off to California!"

I followed her up the stairs and out to the car. She and her mom stowed her gear, buzzing with excitement. They each gave me a hug before they climbed in the car. "Thank you, dear, for keeping Sukey," Mrs. Parsons said.

"Thanks, Paula," Sukey said. "For everything. And for letting me play your guitar." She closed the door.

I wiggled my hands at the window. "Wait, wait, wait. I forgot. I have to get you something."

I dashed into my basement room, grabbed the guitar off the wall, and dashed outside again. I opened the car door with one hand and poked the guitar in with the other. "Here, you take it."

"Oh, no," Sukey said. "That was your birthday present."

"Now it's yours. I can't even sing, remember."

She looked down at the guitar and rubbed her hand over its shiny surface. She wanted it, I knew.

"We can send it back when your daddy buys another one," Mrs. Parsons suggested.

"Okay," Sukey agreed, giving me a sweet smile. "I won't forget you, Paula."

"I won't forget you either."

She pulled the door closed. Her mom started up the motor and they were off. I walked back in the house, trying not to cry.

Paula's Song

Grandma came home before Mom did. She dumped her stuff on a chair and sat heavily down on the couch where I was watching TV. "Sukey's gone," I said.

Grandma murmured, "Hmmm," and absently petted Bitsey, who had jumped into her lap.

"Sukey and her mom left for California today," I said more loudly.

"Oh. You'll be missing her."

"I already do."

Grandma didn't seem to hear me.

I switched off the TV. "What's the matter with you?"

It seemed to take a minute for my question to register in Grandma's head. Then she sucked in a long breath before she answered. "I'm being transferred to an empty school to do inventory."

"For how long?"

"For the rest of the year."

"Then what?"

"Oh, they'll find little jobs for me until I retire."

"You're not going to be a classroom teacher anymore?"

"No, nobody wants me." She sagged back on the couch and Bitsey crawled up her chest and licked her chin with a tiny pink tongue.

"Bitsey wants you," I said.

Two tears rolled down Grandma's cheeks and on down the hanging folds under her jaw. She looked old, awfully old and beaten.

"You wanted a job without students." After I said that, I wished I hadn't. Maybe this wasn't the time to remind her.

She didn't get cross, though. She just said, "You're better at wishing than I am."

"Not really. Sukey smelled when she came. And I didn't like her hogging the rocker. And I was jealous on my birthday when she got all the attention. But, Grandma, I gave her my guitar when she left."

Grandma placed her wrinkled hand over mine. "You're my granddaugher."

When Mom came in, I let Grandma tell her story first. Mom sat on the couch with us and listened with a frown between her eyebrows. Mom frowned so much that even when she wasn't concentrating, the dent stayed above her nose. I wanted to reach my hand up and smooth it away. If she didn't stay pretty, she was never going to get another man.

"But, Mother," Mom said, "will you keep your place on the salary schedule?"

"Yes, but if I'm not teaching Home Ec, I won't get the extra vocational money."

"Well, that's not very much." Mom patted Grandma's arm. "You're going to be all right."

"Sukey's gone," I said.

"Gone? Where?" Mom had switched around on the couch and was staring at me.

"She and her mom have gone to California. Her dad sent them a hundred and twenty dollars and they took off this afternoon."

"After all that business about her glasses?"

I shrugged. "I guess."

Mom's frown got even deeper. "Mrs. Parsons owes me money."

"I know. I've got it." I took it out of my pocket and handed it to her. "Seventy dollars."

Mom counted it and then smiled first at Grandma,

then at me. "Ladies, what do you say we go out for dinner?"

Dad always goes out to dinner. Mom hardly ever does. This time she let me have an Italian soda and ordered wine for herself and Grandma.

The wine made her eyes shine. "What happened to that boyfriend you brought home?" I asked her.

She tipped her head to the side. "We-ell, he was a little scrawny."

"It's hard to get someone as big as Dad."

"Your father is a handsome man," Grandma said.

Mom twirled her wine glass dreamily. "Yes, too bad I couldn't put a sack over his head whenever he left the house."

This kind of talk made me squirm. When your parents split, it isn't easy to keep loyal to both of them. "I wonder if I'll have a nightmare tonight now that Sukey's gone," I said.

"Do you have nightmares when you're alone in the basement?" Mom asked.

"Sometimes." I glanced at Grandma to see if she was going to call me a scaredy-cat, but she didn't.

She said, "Maybe you'll get your old room back. The new place where I'll be working is in south Seattle. The long ride every day might be too much for me. I may have to get an apartment in the south end."

"We can see how that goes later," Mom said. "Right now let's decide what we're having for dessert."

I took chocolate mud pie. Grandma and Mom had cheesecake. That night when I went to bed I only had a small nightmare, thinking I heard three knocks on my window.

In the morning, it seemed strange to get up without Sukey. At school, Mr. Loyal and the kids wanted to know where she was. Every few days, one of them would ask me if I'd heard from her and I'd have to say no.

"Who cares," Karen said.

Mr. Loyal heard her and told us it was talented people like Sukey who made old acquaintances brag about having known her once.

That shut Karen up.

Two Saturdays after Sukey left, I was in my room changing my bed when I heard the kitchen door open and Mom tell someone, "Take this down to her."

Casey came into my room holding a letter. "It's from Sukey."

I snatched the letter from him and ripped open the envelope. "What'd she say?" Casey asked.

"I'll read it to you." I settled on my half-made bed before I started.

"Hi Paula, We made it to San Francisco. Mom's old clunk burned oil all the way. Daddy's place is only a room about half as big as yours.

"I don't mind. I play your guitar all day. I'm not going to school until we get an apartment. We're staying here because we have to save up the first and last month's rent for one.

"Guess what? I finished 'The Traveling Song' and now I'm writing 'Paula's Song.' Maybe when Mom gets her job, I can send you a tape of it. Maybe for Christmas.

"Say hi to everyone for me. Especially your grandma and Casey. Love ya, Sukey.

"Gee, Casey. She remembered you."

Casey flipped two marker pens into the air and caught them one by one. "I thought you wanted me to draw on your wall."

"I do. I do."

"Take down that mule then. I'll make a good one."

"No, don't draw another mule. Draw me something to remind me of Sukey."

"I don't know. That might be lot of work. I might get hungry."

"I'll make you lunch." I bounced off the bed and up the stairs.

The only bread we had was in the freezer. By the time I had it defrosted and the sandwiches made, Casey was almost finished outlining his drawing in pencil. I peered over the lunch tray. "Casey! That's a horse!"

"Relax, Paula. I'm not finished yet."

I tried to relax while I ate my sandwich. Casey ate his while he worked on the wall. He was taking so long I finished making my bed and hauled my sheets up to the washer. I stopped at the counter to see what Grandma was making. "Oh, chocolate-chip cookies. Casey'll love those."

Downstairs Casey backed away from the wall. "Okay! What do you think?"

There was a huge black horse trotting toward distant hills. Riding the horse was a girl with a guitar hanging down her back. The girl had long, dark brown hair and slanted eyes.

"It's Sukey!" I said. "Traveling Sukey. Oh, Casey, I love it!"

I pulled Grandma and Mom downstairs to admire the drawing.

"I guess we know what you're going to be when you grow up," Mom said to Casey.

"A tattoo artist like my dad," Casey said.

"I'd better get my cookies out of the oven," Grandma said.

"Cookies!" Casey said.

That night I fell asleep with my light on. I'd been looking at my wall, wondering if someday I'd say I knew Sukey, wondering what the words to "Paula's Song" would be.